The Pagoda

by Nariyuki Koda
[Rohan Kōda]

I0682943

Translated from the Japanese by
Sakae Shioya

Zea Books
Lincoln, Nebraska
2022

Written by Rohan Kōda and published 1891-92.
This English translation published by Tokyo Okura & Co. in 1909.
Sakae Shioya (1873–1961) was the author of *When I Was a Boy in Japan* (Boston, 1906).

ISBN 978-1-60962-241-1   paperback
ISBN 978-1-60962-242-8   ebook
doi: 10.32873/unl.dc.zea.1321

Zea Books are published by the University of Nebraska-Lincoln Libraries.

Electronic (pdf) edition available online at
https://digitalcommons.unl.edu/zeabook/

Print edition available from Lulu.com at
http://www.lulu.com/spotlight/unllib

THE PAGODA

I

By the side of a strong-looking rectangular fire-box made of beautifully grained elm and rimmed designedly with red oak sat a woman of about thirty, without anyone to talk with. Her fine mannish eyebrows had been shaved, leaving bluish traces fresh as the hue of distant hills after the rain; her nose was straight, her eyes obliquely set; and though her recently washed hair was ruthlessly coiled round a hair-pin with the help of a torn slip of paper—a plain toilet, to be sure—a lock or two of that soft, midnight hair, hanging loose about her rather dark yet pretty face, she appeared decidedly lovely and might easily be an object of admiration, even to those who believed that beauty was a thing of the past with a woman of her age. Indeed, she was so attractive that some idle fellow on seeing her might be induced to think vainly of some fancy garments he would like to see her in, were she his sweetheart. But what she put on was far on the side of soberness, with no regard for its appearance. The pattern of her dress was, indeed, not bad to look at, but it was all cotton, quilted and collared with a piece of black satin, and without any touch of brightness.

The broadly striped coat she had on was some old thing, though silk; one cannot tell how many times it had been sent to washing.

In the kitchen the noise of a maid washing dishes was heard. But for that the house was quiet, and no one else seemed to be about. The woman, who was dallying with a tooth-pick in her mouth, now bit it off and spat it out. Levelling the ashes of the fire-box, she buried the burnt charcoal and taking out a rag from a basket, polished the silvery iron work. And after wiping the copper, clearing the lid of the boiler, and placing securely a large iron pot, she reached with a tortoise-shell pipe for a small mosaic tobacco-box, probably a sou-venir from Hakone. Drawing in the smoke leisurely and puffing it out slowly like the burning of incense sticks, she heaved a sigh unwittingly and mused in this way:

"Probably it will come into the hands of Genta. But they say that that detestable slouch, forgetting our favour in giving him work last year, tried to rival my husband and, flattering the Abbot, applied for the work. The Abbot may be prejudiced by him, but to give the important work to a man of little name like that slouch will be impossible in the face of the parishioners and contributors. And so it is certain that we shall get the order. And then, even if the case is reversed, the work is too much for that fellow, and as he can hardly get good carpenters under him, it is very clear that he will utterly fail. So says Seikichi. But I wish Genta would come back soon and tell me smiling that he has the order at last. This kind of work, he says, is rather rare, and so he wants to do it by all means, gain or no gain. He wishes to be known as the builder of the pagoda at the Kannoji Temple, Yanaka, and be lauded for his work. Spurred with the idea, he goes about his business these days with more spirit than ever. And so if he is not successful, you can't tell how much he will get provoked. That is perfectly natural, and I see no way of consoling him. But for mercy's sake, let me see his happy face soon."

Thus she waited anxiously for her husband, who went out that morning, putting on with her help a coat of her own tailoring, when some one opened the front lattice-door roughly.

"Is boss in?" the man asked at the door.

"Gone to the Kannoji? Well, there is no help then. I am sorry 1 must ask of your favour, ma'am. I tippled a little last night, and ....."

The rest he did not say, but let his peculiar gestures tell. On this the woman drew her eyebrows a little and, smiling, said:

"Shame on you! But take a little more care to be sober, Seikichi."

She rose and handed him some money. Seikichi went out with it, and after carrying on
some negotiation with somebody who waited
outside, returned, and placing his fist on his
brow, bowed thanks awkwardly.

II

"Come near the fire-box, as I shan't go into the trouble of making you a separate warmer," said the woman and moved the iron pot heavily, and, amiable to her inferior, made him a cup of cured cherry-flowers. Hospitality, given with truly obliging heart, is more enjoyable than fair words. And Seikichi now had it. But because his shameless request had been complied with, agreeably, and because in the frank treatment now accorded him there was nothing unusual, he became rather ashamed of his deed and felt something mortifying in a corner of his soul. He could hardly reach his arm for shame to take up his cup, and, after bowing and making apology twice, he could wet his parched tongue at last. The woman soon broke the silence.

"You seem to have been petted too much last night, judging from your late coming back," she laughed. "I don't say anything against dissipation, but, Seikichi, isn't it a shame to let your mother worry about you by neglecting your work? I understand you have been ordered to engage now in making a tea-room at the villa of Negishi soon after you finished building the house of Koshuya at Nakacho. My husband is also much addicted to dissipation at times, and would revel, taking the lead of you fellows, but he hates to slight his business. He is sure to fire up when he sees you. Of course, you know this, don't you? Well, it's pretty late now, but you had better go to Negishi. You might easily excuse yourself by saying that your mother has been ill, or something of that sort. The overseer there is a good man, and, seeing that you do not fool away a whole day, even if he guesses the truth, will not report ill of you to my husband. Oh, you haven't yet had your breakfast. Say, San, set the table for Seikichi there. We can't treat you to boiled bean-cake and stewed clams, but you don't mind baked beans and new pickles, do you? Have two or three bowls of rice and run to your work at once. Ha, ha; you feel sleepy! But you can very well bear it if you think of last night. Don't be indolent. Your lunch? Don't trouble yourself about it; we'll let Matsu take it for you."

Seikichi, honest at heart, sweated and felt sorry for his misdemeanour under her mild yet effective chiding.

"Then I shall avail myself of your kindness and hurry to my work immediately," said he, and moping his brow with a handkerchief, went to the kitchen. In no time he finished five or six bowls of rice and came out.

"I am going. Sayonara," said he and bowed. With the impetuosity of the true Yedo people, he now put his pipe in the case, fixed his tobacco-pouch on his belt, and, slipping on his sandals, went out.

At this moment the woman, who had been silent till now, suddenly called him back with such spark-like vehemence in her voice, and asked if he met the slouch. Seikichi turned about.

"Yes, I met him," said he. "I saw him only yesterday at Gotenzaka, hanging his head like a dead chicken and walking slowly, more like a fool than ever. Though there is no doubt of his failure in rivalling with my master and in hoping what is beyond such a dullard as he, it drove me mad to think he was the cause of some anxiety to you and my master. And so I insulted him by calling names. Of course, he was not aware of me at first. Again I called him, and, at the third time, I roared near his ear, when at last he woke up, and, staring me like an owl, answered me in a drowsy voice, 'Well, Seikichi!' 'Look here,' said I sarcastically, 'you got to be quite ambitious, didn't you? It seems you went up in a dream a drying stand on the top of a dyer's house, for I hear you want to build quite a tall thing and is begging the Abbot of the Kannoji to let you do it. Now, are you doing it awake or a-dreaming?' But a dullard is generally honest, isn't he? I wondered what he would answer. Why, he said that he did not spare any trouble to beg of it, but found it quite painful to run against our boss. So he wished that the boss would kindly give it over to him. What a self-interested idea! But it makes me laugh to think of his serious look when he said it anxiously. It was so ridiculous that I forgot to hate him. And I left him calling him stick."

"Is it all?"

"Yes."

"Is it? Well, you will be late. You may go at once."

"Sayonara," said Seikichi once more. And as he went to his work, the woman, left alone, fell to musing.

Outside, guileless children were heard engaging noisily in a top-fight. They shouted and screamed. A voice said: "One knock; two knocks. There! Take my revenge, you dog!" Surely this is a world of struggle for existence.

III

A woman of about twenty-five, not so plain, yet pale and slightly pock-marked, and looking somewhat dry, sat at her sewing in a miserable room, making herself appear still more miserable for the neglect of her toilet and for her dress worn to rags. She was heard to soliloquize:

"Well-to-do people take no thought for the coming of winter and putting on what silk dresses they like, have no sympathy with the poor who do not know how to provide for it. And making a stir of such a thing as the day to start tea ceremony, they hurry workmen to finish the tea-rooms by all means in time and to mend the eaves of the waiting-room, and, saying that the noise of the night rain pattering on the window door is not enjoyable by hearing it without sipping tea, they think the winter of bleak wind and frosty temple bells, gradually becoming colder and drearer, as something pleasant. But poor workmen, freezing their hands in whetting planes to smooth the floor boards of the tea-rooms, or falling sick by over-exposure in erecting fences — for what guilt committed in the pre-existing world do they now suffer unlike others? And especially this is so with my husband, who is good-natured but most

unconversant among his fellow workmen in
the way of the world. Though his workmanship is so fine and even secured praises of
Genta-sama when he did some work for him
last year, he is so ungrudging as to miss nice
jobs and is always fooled by others. Indeed,
it disheartens me to think that thus we have
to lead such an unhappy life. As a wife I feel
ashamed to let my husband wear the same
old pair of pants with mended patches at the
knees. But there may be no help for it, as all is
from our being badly off. These striped pieces
I am now sewing to make a dress for my boy,
Ino, have been washed many times and are
faded. And not only all my pains to make it
look nice can hardly be rewarded, but, on the
contrary, new stitches make it appear all the
more shabby. But some time since, innocent
Ino came and said: 'Ma, whose dress is that?
It must be mine as it is small. How glad I am
of it!' And he went out happy and delighted,
and wanted to chase this lovely afternoon red
dragon-flies flying in the air with a bamboo
stick. But how far is he gone now? Oh, I hate
to sit gloomily at sewing like this. If my husband were half as clever in his business as he
is skilful in his work, we should not be in such
a strait. He has ability, but it is like treasure
kept to no purpose, as they say. Having no
occasion to show it to the eyes of the world,
he does not seem to differ from a mere nail-

driving carpenter, and they call him by the abominable nickname of slouch and make light of him in every way. How it tortures me and drives me mad to think of it.

"He was indifferent altogether in spite of all that I feel for him. But surely I cannot understand what passes in his mind this time. No sooner had he heard the project to build a pagoda at the Kannoji than he suddenly wanted to do the work at any cost. I wished him to wake up. But certainly this is not the way he should do. It is mean to forget the kindness of Genta-sama and try to seize what he desires to get. Besides, the work itself is too much for a man of our means to undertake. So it seems even to me, and I don't know how people will scandalize him about it. Naturally Genta-sama must be in a rage, and still more so with O-Kichi-sama. My husband went out this morning to see the Abbot, as this is the day he is most likely to decide which of the two the work shall be intrusted to. He has not come back yet. But so far as this work is concerned, however my husband may desire it, as it is beyond our means and as we are bound to respect Genta-sama's wish, I feel as if I would rather have the Abbot give it to Genta-sama. But, of course, if Genta-sama is large-minded and does not take it in bad part, I feel as if I would rather have Jubei undertake the hard work and finish it successfully.

Oh, how uneasy I am! I wonder how the matter will come out. I hardly think the Abbot will entrust the work to my husband, but in case he should, how much will Genta-sama and O-Kichi-sama resent? Oh, dear, how my head aches! If my husband finds this out, he will again give me a gentle but unreasonable lecture that I trouble myself with useless womanish anxiety, and so I am always sickly. Well, let me stop, let me stop. But oh, my head!"

Saying this she dropped the piece she was sewing, with wry faces, and with both hands pressed her plastered temples, when an old paper screen, separating the kitchen, was heard suddenly to open.

"Ma, look here," said Ino. Surprised she turned and asked how long he had been there, when she saw a mimic pagoda the boy had erected by piling up small pieces of board! The mother was in tears at the sight before she knew, and, all at once, took Ino into her arms, sobbing:

"O my good boy!"

IV

The Kannoji Temple of Yanaka built by the then famous architect, Gentaro Kawagoye, was above criticism in every respect as might be expected. The chapel thirty feet square with the latticed ceiling, the long bridge-like verandah, the guests' rooms, the chamber of the Abbot, the tea-room, the rooms for the monks and postulants, the kitchen, the bath-room and the hall—all were finished splendidly or solidly, gaily or softly, each admirably suited to its use and leaving nothing to wish for. But who is the man that raised such a fine edifice out of an old small thing? He is Abbot Royen of Uda, so well known at the time that a child, on hearing his pious name, is said to have joined hands and prayed. From youth he was at the temple on Mount Minobu, devoting himself to the study of the teachings of Buddha afterwards bore the hardship of a long pilgrimage throughout the land; and, edified through privation and meditation, was long preaching the way to salvation. He was over seventy, lean as a stork for his simple living, and looking half dreamy as if aweary of human discord. Knowing the vanity of things, he was not disturbed by any covetous desire, and, believing in the truth of nirvana, he kept his mind free from worldly ambition.

So it was not in his desire primarily to build temples and edifices. But as many novices came to him, hearing his name and desiring to study under him, the old temple got to be too small to give them shelter. And he was heard once murmuring to himself that he wished that the place were a little larger, when the report quickly got wind to the effect that the pious Abbot wanted a new temple on a larger plan. Soon some clever disciples canvassed round of their own accord for the fund, and some parishioners, too, made a point of making the rich interested in the enterprise by telling them about the virtuous life of the Abbot. Many were the people who always revered and looked up to him, that this made a great stir among them, and all from nobles down to merchants contributed for the pious cause gold, silver, or copper according to their means, and strove to reap happiness in the next world, by sowing the seed of good deed. The money, pouring in like streams into the sea, reached in a short time to a wonderful amount. Then proper officers being elected, the work of building the temple was carried on to a successful end.

But, on the day of completion when Treasurer Tameyemon settled the accounts, he found a large amount of money still remaining unused. A meeting was called in which the officers with shaven heads and unshaven heads, with Monk Endo as chairman, consulted as to its proper use, but they could not hit a good idea. It might be applied to the buying of land, but plenty of land had already been contributed, and there was no use of expending this consecrated fund for that purpose. The Abbot would not trouble himself in such a small matter, but one day Monk Endo took liberty to ask his opinion, when the Abbot said just one word; "Build a pagoda with it," and, without doing so much as to turn and see him, was reading on silently some scripture, through a pair of large tortoise-shell-rimmed spectacles.

A pagoda was to be build. And Monk Endo ordered Genta to send in an estimate of it, when Jubei, better known by the name of "slouch," — how he heard of it no one could tell — suddenly called to see the Abbot. It was about two months before.

V

With his hair gray with dust and his face sunburnt, and putting on a pair of old patched pants and a coat once dark blue but now weathered and discoloured with sweat and washing, and with letters once white on the collar, becoming dim, an unprepossessing fellow, made still more so by such negligence, was entering awkwardly the gate of the Kannoji Temple. On being questioned sharply by the porter, who he was, he stared a while surprisingly, and then bending his body, said very politely:

"I am Jubei, the carpenter. I have come, on the business of the new erection."

The porter was somewhat suspicious of his faltering manner, but, thinking he must be one of Genta's men as he said he was a carpenter, allowed him haughtily to pass. Encouraged by this, Jubei, looking about him, drew near the stately porch. He asked for admittance once, twice, thrice, when a neat little boy with a blue shaved head and in a gray gown, answered him and opened the door. But perceiving at once what sort of man the caller was, the little door-keeper, without coming down a step as in receiving a guest, or doing so much as to bend his knees, said:

"Go to the rear if you are on business." And he shut the door coldly upon him. Nothing was now heard but the voices of bulbuts singing on a tree somewhere.

"Indeed!" said Jubei to himself and went round to the back door and again asked for admittance, when Secretary Tameyemon came out, looking grave and censorious.

"I am sure I don't know you, but from where and for what did you come?" asked he, already making light of the man for his poor dress.

But Jubei, not minding it, said lowly:

"I am Jubei, the carpenter. I want to see the Abbot on business and wish you would kindly tell him so."

Tameyemon stared at him and surveyed him contemptuously from the top of his dirty head to the tips of his dusty feet in old sandals.

"No," said he; "no, I can't. The Abbot does not trouble himself with ordinary business. But," continued he as if he was in the habit of managing everything by himself, "tell me about whatever it may be. I may arrange it for you."

"No, thank you," said the simple-minded Jubei bluntly, indifferent to his seeming kindness. "No, thank you; unless I can see the Abbot in person, there is no use of telling about it to anybody. So just take me to him, if you please."

"You dull-brained fellow," said Tame-yemon feeling hurt at being made light of, "I told you the Abbot will not give an ear to workmen like you, and it is useless to tell him of your coming. So I said I might arrange anything with you. But how dare you be so insolent as to ignore my kindness? I will not see you any longer. Now go back, go back."

As is usual with narrow-minded people, Tameyemon got easily worked up into a passion, and with these rough words, was about to turn coldly away, when Jubei, agitated, stammered:

"But —"

"Shut up, you noisy dog!"

With this stunning word, he disappeared, and Jubei stood alone bewildered, feeling as if a fire-worm he thought he palmed had slipped away. There being no help now, he again asked for admittance. The large temple being cold and silent, only the echo fell on his ears, and even a sound of coughing was not heard within. He went back to the porch and asked once more when that cunning looking boy just put out his face and, muttering "I told you to go to the rear," shut the screen with a slam.

Jubei went again to the kitchen and came back to the porch, and again repeated the process, and at last, forgetting his reserve, he shouted with a voice that might reach to the inner chapel:

"Isn't anybody in?"

"You, fool!" A louder voice was heard to answer, and Tameyemon came out. "Drag this madcap out of the gate, boys. We shall get scolded on account of this fellow. The Abbot dislikes a noise."

"All right, sir," said a chorus of boys who waited in their rooms, and who at once set about the task. Jubei squatted on the ground and held to it, while the boys made a great noise raising him up. At this moment, Abbot Royen, — he had been looking round in the garden for some flowers he wanted for his room — dressed in nut-brown, and holding some golden-rods and bluebells in his left hand, and a pair of scissors with red handles in his right, happened to come to the spot.

VI

"What is the matter?"

The Abbot spoke, and his voice fell on the mob like that of a stork on chattering sparrows, and the noise ceased at once. Some lost chance to hide their upraised fists, and stood like a duck in thunder; some were awkwardly straightening their tucked-up sleeves, and, by stealth, went behind others. And Tameyemon, whose upturned nostrils seemed to throw up a fume of arrogant rage, now hung his head and rubbed his hands as if in shame. But, being himself a ringleader, he reported on the matter, giving a colour to his part as much as possible, when the Abbot, deepening the wrinkles furrowed in his lean face, smiled meekly and, with a voice soft and gentle like that of a woman's, said:

"Then you have no cause for such ado. If you had only told me of his coming as he wished, Tameyemon, you would not have had any trouble. Well, Jubei, — if I got your name right — come after me. I feel very sorry we maltreated you so."

The man who is looked up to by thousands has a peculiar way of his own: he does not hold the lowly and the ignorant in contempt, but is always gentle and considerate to them.

And so was the Abbot, and Jubei, dull-brained as he was, could not but be moved to tears at his kindness.

He now followed after the Abbot, and, passing on in turn over the places where red earth lay moist, where stepping stones were laid picturesquely, and where shadows of slender aogiri fell dark and the bamboo leaves grew green, he entered by a wicket a small secluded garden, now destitute of flowers and looking lonesome, and where a hexagonal white paper lantern strewn over with some fallen pine needles, and a stone water-basin overgrown with moss, added to the note of unearthliness.

The Abbot went up, leaving his clogs on the stepping stone.

"Come up, Jubei," said he, putting the flowers he had in his hand in a hanging flower vase. Jubei did not hesitate, and, being too careless to dust his feet, went at once into a small tea-room awkwardly. Sitting very close to the Abbot, he silently made a bow clumsy but bespeaking his honest heart. Striving many times in vain to speak, he at last opened his heavy lips and stammered:

"About the pagoda … I wanted to see you about the pagoda."

It sounded as if it dropped from the clouds, and as Jubei, sitting like a frog and shaky in his voice, finished it with difficulty, with the beads of perspiration standing on his brow, the Abbot laughed unwittingly.

"Don't think me as something frightful," he said. "I don't know what you say, but tell me at length without any reserve. It seems you have something you thought out deeply, judging from the way you squatted and held to the ground. Now, don't make haste but think of me as your friend and tell me about it fully."

Jubei, easily moved, moistened his large owl-like eyes.

"Yes; I thank you," said he. "I have something I thought out deeply. It is about the pagoda. I am, as you see, a sort of fellow called by such a bad name as slouch. But I assure you, Abbot, I am not unskilled. I know I am a fool; I am fooled; I am not smart. But I don't lie, Abbot, I do good work. I am used to Osumi style from boyhood, but I am thoroughly competent in Goto and Tatekawa styles, too. Give me … I wish you to give me the work of building the new pagoda. I have come for it. I heard a few days ago that Genta-sama of Kawagoye had sent in his estimate. I haven't slept since, Abbot. The building of a pagoda happens only once in a hundred years, — once in our life time. I don't want to snatch the work from Genta-sama whom I am much indebted to. I envy clever people. Genta-sama is lucky to do the work that comes only once in our life time, in a hundred years. And he will be remembered after his death for his fine work. I feel very envious of it. Life is worth while for him as carpenter. But as for me, though I don't think I am by any mistake behind anybody, not even Genta-sama, in point of workmanship, I am destined to do all the year round such a petty work as the mending of weather boarding of tenements, or the making of gutters of stables, I have resigned meekly to my fate, because Heaven has not been pleased to give me sagacity. But as often as I see unskilled fellows get contracts for temples and shrines and erect what, seen with eyes that can see, makes us feel sorry for those for whom they have been built, I weep over my poor lot. Sometimes I feel like hating those fellows who are only sagacious without being skilful. But I am really envious of Genta-sama, because he is sagacious as well as skilful, and does fine work. O me! O lucky Genta-sama! O, woe is me! So I cried one night and went to bed weeping, without even speaking a word to my wife. While I lay, I saw some fearful-looking being who commanded me: 'Build a pagoda; build it at once!' Surprised I jumped out of bed and thrust my hand into my tool-box. I remembered it half real and half visionary. But when I woke up completely, to my great disappointment, I was only lying down, hurting the tip of my finger with a chisel, and holding a side of my box. Then I sat lonely before the dim light and regretted that it was only a dream. Do you understand, Abbot, how I felt? Do you understand me? If anybody could only understand me that much, I might as well give up the idea of building a pagoda. Being such a fool, I would not care to die. I would not have to live like a worn-out tool. I tell you, Abbot, since that night whether I looked up to the clear sky or in a dark corner of my room, I saw plainly a small pagoda finished in white wood, standing and staring at me! At last I wanted to materialize it. Incapable as I was, I set about every evening after the day's work, to make a model of one-fiftieth size all through the night, and finished it last evening. I wish you would come to see it, Abbot. Yes, I finished the work I was not asked to do, but I am not given the work I want to do. As I was grieving over my hard lot, my wife said, shaking the model, that if I had not been able to finish it, I should not have known how hard my lot was. It was too true, and I wept more for that. For mercy's sake, Abbot, let me build the new pagoda. I pray you thus."

And Jubei joined his hands, bowed his head low, and wetted the mat with tears.

VII

The Abbot sat silent as a wooden image of Rakan, and, telling the beads of a linden rosary, lent an ear to the confused talk of Jubei.

"I understand," said he, stopping Jubei from making the bow; "I understand you well. You have such a fine spirit. I am all but moved to tears. I wish all my scholars here would learn of you. I will go by all means to see the model you mentioned. But though I feel proud of you, I wish to make it clear that I cannot be so rash as to entrust you arbitrarily the work of building the pagoda. Whether we will let you have the work or not, the decision will be sent to you officially from the Kannoji and not from me. At any rate, I wish to see the model, and as I am free to-day, you will take me to your house now."

While the modest Abbot spoke thus clearly and with discrimination, Jubei, his face all smiles, bowed his head repeatedly like a pestle pounding rice, and was saying all the while, "Yes, sir."

"You will consider my request," he now said encouraged. "I thank you very much. And are you coming to my house? I cannot bear to cause you such a trouble. I will bring the model at once. Excuse me."

Dull as he was, he was not same as usual for joy, and no sooner did he make an exaggerated bow than he ran off, stumbling at stepping stones. And returning to his house, and without even speaking to his surprised wife, he took out the model in no time, and, getting a help, carried it to the Kannoji with a breathless speed. He then set it before the Abbot and returned.

On careful inspection, the Abbot saw that the proportion of the stories from the first to the fifth, the inclination of the roofs and the eaves, the height of the wainscots, the arrangement of the rafters and the appearance of more minute parts of the work — all showed a delicate and tasteful workmanship, and left nothing to wish for. And it was surprising that such a marvel of perfection was produced from the hands of such a clumsy looking fellow as he.

As he admired it, the Abbot thought that it was a great pity that the man, master of the art as he was, remained buried in oblivion and had no chance to make his name.

"Even a stranger," he continued in his mind, "feels very sorry for such a man; how unendurable, then, would it be for him to think of his own lot? And nothing would exceed the pleasure of helping him get distinguished and accomplish what he has long sought for. Men who perish like weeds are but transitory; we cannot help their vanishing away; our regret will be of no avail. Yes, the art of carpentry is insignificant. But he who puts his whole heart into the work, and, thinking life itself of little importance before the task, takes his sole delight in the perfection of his art, — he has a mind more precious than gold or silver. To think that it should be quitted without leaving anything to remind of it, and that it should only be carried away to the nether world! His lot will not be very much different from that of a noble soul barred from accomplishing his mission. Good! I chanced to see a gleam of the precious gem in Jubei's bosom. That was fortunate. We will then let him have the work of building the pagoda this time, and reap the fruits of his honest efforts. But wait, I know Genta Kawagoye desires specially to get the work, too. He is the one who built the temple, and then he has already sent in his estimate for the work. I examined it a few days ago. Genta cannot be said unskilled; and then he has more credit than Jubei. Two builders for one pagoda! I wish to give it to either of them. What shall I do?"

VIII

"Come to the Kannoji in person by eight o'clock to-morrow morning. The Abbot is going to speak to you about the building of the pagoda, the work you have requested to get a contract for. Be careful of your dress in coming."

So spoke Enchin, the messenger, studiedly at the house of Genta. He was a humourous-looking monk with a red-tipped nose he was served out with, for his undue fondness for red pepper. Genta used to see him every day while building the temple, and got intimate enough to cut jokes and to call him by the nickname of 'Dutchman' (on account of his nose). But he had not seen him much of late, and to-day Enchin gave himself airs of a messenger monk, and was carefully hiding his hands in the long sleeves of his black gown — the hands with the index and middle fingers of which, he was in the habit of scratching the top of his shaved helmet-like head. So Genta bowed with respect and gave him his formal consent. O-Kichi, however, as if wanting her husband to be well spoken of even by such a petty monk, made a small package of the cakes he had left untouched, together with some coins, and let him take it on his departure. A clever way of making gratuity, to be sure.

Enchin went then to the house of Jubei, and saying the same thing, returned. On the day following, Genta, shaved and neatly dressed, went to the Kannoji in high spirits, thinking that the Abbot would be glad to give him the work that day, and being made to wait in a certain room, stayed there sitting up straight. Now, Jubei, though different in outward appearance, came equally excited and was shown to another room. He waited there alone, anxious for some one to take him to the Abbot. "Will he say to me, 'I will entrust you, with the building of the pagoda and all the work connected with it?'" he asked of himself: "or is not this, by any chance, to reject my application as the result of the work being turned over to Genta? What shall I do if that be the case? I am then doomed never to bloom, like a tree buried in the ground. Would that the Abbot for pity's sake were pleased to give me the work!"

Thus Jubei, unconscious of beautiful gold and silver phoenixes painted on the nine feet of screens before him, was for a while musing wanderingly as if groping in the dark, when that smart-looking boy came in and said:

"The Abbot is going to see you. Please come this way."

Jubei felt uneasy as he followed the usher, thinking that at last the critical moment at which his wish would be granted or rejected was drawing near. He was now led to a room and was entering it after the boy, when unexpectedly he saw someone inside cast at him a glance fiery with anger. It was Genta, and not a shadow of the Abbot was to be found. Surprised Jubei stopped short, staring at Genta without a word. But as nothing could be done, he at last sat down at about twice the width of a mat from him, and hanging down his dejected head, looked only at his knees sadly. Genta, on the contrary, proud like an eagle on a high cliff, daring the wind and looking down at his prey, sat straight and high-mettled, and not bending his back or lowering his shoulders. He looked fine and carried himself so splendidly that no one could help admiring him.

The Abbot, who was not biased with outward appearance, and who always looked through the clear spectacles of his mind unstained with worldly views, loved both men for different reasons, and was unable to make a choice for the work till yesterday. But today, for some reason or other, he wanted to see them and had them both wait in the same room. He now came quietly out of his chamber, and stepping softly, entered the room as a page opened the screen. As he took his seat, both men bowed together with great respect, and were unable to raise their heads for a while. When the salutation was over, Jubei was blushing with bashfulness, poor fellow! like a timid country boy facing a royal prince: the wrinkles, furrowed deep in his forehead, were brimming with hot sweat, and the tip of his nose oozed out briny beads, while his bony fingers on his knees, though rough and stout like dead pine branches, were all shaking. With such a feeling of fear, he faced the moment when a word dropped from the Abbot's mouth would decide his fate. And Genta, too, remained speechless and waited for the Abbot to speak, straining his ears.

The Abbot, who could read the hearts of these two men equally worthy of sympathy, could not easily find any chance to open his mouth, and was silent for a while.

"Now, listen to me, Genta and Jubei," said he at last. "The pagoda we are going to build is only one, while we have you two who desire to get the work. I wish I could give it to both of you, but you know this is impossible. Of course, if I entrust it to one of you, the other will be greatly disappointed. We have, however, no standard to go by in making our choice. Our officers could not decide, nor could I either. So I will place the matter wholly in your hands. I have no objection whichever way you agree to. I will take up your decision, so you go back and find out the best way. This is all I have to say, and I want you understand me rightly. You may go back now, but as I am at leisure to-day and have nothing diverting, I wish you to stay for a while, and have a talk with me over the tea. I want you to tell me about something stirring in the outside world. I came across some amusing old stories yesterday, and shall tell them to you."

And the Abbot smiled and treated both as if they were his good friends.

IX

As the Abbot poured the tea the boy had brought, and served it himself to the two men, they felt extremely honoured and received it with utmost courtesy.

"I can't talk familiarly with you," said the Abbot, "if you are so reserved; my words would never get rid off corners. I shall not pass the cakes, so you will help yourselves to them."

Thus saying, he pushed the lacquered cake plate towards them, and taking up his cup, wetted his throat.

"Not being a man of the world," he went on, "I don't have many interesting stories, but I came across quite an interesting one the other day, in the scripture I was reading. This is the story; I want you to hear me.

"Once there was an elderly man in a certain country, who went one fine morning to take a walk with his two boys, in a field green with soft grass and fragrant with lovely flowers. He came to a large river with its water low, as it was early summer, yet clear and sparkling along the bank. There was a beautiful strand in the river, of pearline pebbles and silvery sand. The elderly man was charmed at the sight, and jumping with ease over a belt of water about a fathom wide, landed on it. As he looked about, he found that the place was also separated on the other side by a stream of about equal width. It was a clear, unearthly spot, totally isolated from the filthy soil of the world. He was overjoyed to be on it, but taking pity on the two boys who could not come, and who were only crying to be helped over, said:

"'This is too hallowed a place for you, but I will help you come over if you wait a little bit. Look at these pebbles at my feet; they are rare ones, being all shaped like lotus-flowers. And this remarkable sand; it gives lustres of precious metals.'

"At this the two boys were all the more spurred to get over, but their father held them back quietly till he bridged the stream with a fallen palm-tree uprooted by flood. Then the brothers, each wanting to get ahead, had a quarrel. The elder one, however, being naturally stronger, threw down his brother, and elated with selfish success, stepped hurriedly on the log. But no sooner was he on the middle of it than the younger one sprung up in the heat of passion and shook the bridge. The elder, of course, fell into the stream, and after much struggle, reached the strand. At this moment, the younger brother was seen successfully crossing the bridge, when the elder one lost no time in giving it a shake. Of course, the younger one lost his footing on the log, and was thrown into the river. He, wet and dripping, was barely able to climb up near his father.

"Upon this the father heaved a sigh and said:

"'Now, look here. No sooner did you two step on this place than it was changed all of a sudden: The pebbles got dark and ugly; the sand turned to be a tawny, ordinary thing. Look at them; isn't it true?'

"The two were surprised and examined, open-eyed. There was no mistake about it 'Was it for this that I harmed my dear brother?' each asked of himself, and felt greatly ashamed of his act. And the younger brother wrung out the drenched sleeves of the elder, while the latter did the same with the skirts of the former, and each, taking care of the other, tried to make good his wrong-doing.

"The father, then, dragging the palm-tree to the other side, and bridging the stream, said: 'There is no more use to be here; let's go over. But you two had better go first.'

"The brothers looked at each other, and far from being rude, each asked the other to cross first. The elder brother was made at last to go ahead on account of his age, when the younger one, fearing the unstableness of the bridge, held the end secure. And when the time for the younger brother came, the elder one did the same with it. The father jumped across without any trouble, and the three were enjoying a nice walk. The elder brother now happened to pick up a pebble, which, being shaped like a lotus-flower, the younger one could not help expressing his admiration for, while he himself was surprised to see the sand the younger brother had gathered, emitting the lustres of the precious metals. The brothers were overjoyed, each congratulating the other on his good fortune, when their father, taking a real lotus-flower-shaped gem out of his breast, gave it to the elder son, and also taking genuine gold sand from his sleeve, handed it to the younger son, saying that they should keep them carefully.

"Such is the story, a sort of nursery tale as you hear, but Budhist stories are not mere fictions. If you read them aright, you will find a good deal of interesting teaching in them. How do you like this one? I like it myself very much."

The Abbot ended thus lightly, but the truth of the fable fallen from his lips went into the hearts of the listeners. And Genta and Jubei exchanged looks and remained perplexed.

X

On his way home from the Kannoji, Jubei dragged on, folding his arms under the broad sleeves, and looking half dead. "Dull as I am," mused he, "I can see what the Abbot hinted at. He wanted that one of us should yield meekly to the other. But how I dislike to give this up! I worked nights without sleep, discarding angrily the tender advice of my wife to stop betimes for the cold, planned as best as I could, and fashioned the model with all the skill I had, because I thought that this was the only chance in my life and that I could gladly die if I built what represented the utmost stretch of my power. But pity me for what the Abbot said to-day. It is all truth; I know one ought to act as in the story. But what chance have I to build a pagoda if I miss this? And am I destined after all to pass all my life unknown? Ah me! Would that I were not born! I know perfectly the kind intention of the Abbot, and do not feel a bit ungrateful. But, ah, how hard! And the man I deal with is Chief Genta whom I owe my obligation; how could I bear him a grudge? Then is there no other way for me but to resign meekly? Ah, is there no other way after all? But I cannot be easily reconciled to now. Had I not set my mind upon such a thing and remained satisfied

with being a sluggard, I should not be mortified thus. I was wrong to forget what I am. Indeed, I was wrong. But — no; but — no, let
me think no more. All will be well if I remain
a sluggard and a laughing stock to the clever
in the world. Yes, all will be well if I live on
like a dream and pass away like a dream, de-
plored even by my wife as good-for-nothing.
To be so resolved — ah, I find the world is all
empty now. Fate is too cruel with me. Well,
there! a useless complaint again. Indeed, if I
think carefully over what the Abbot said without alluding plainly, I cannot be but grateful for his boundless kindness, and have no
cause for further grumbling. And in the light
of the sacred story of the two brothers the Abbot told us with the intention of judging the
quarreling two without hurting either one's
feelings, and wishing us to be friendly now
as ever, I stand naturally for the part of the
younger brother, and unless I resign, I am no
better than a brute. Oh, how hard is the lot of
the younger brother!"

His eyes dim with tears of dejection and
unable to see the road he trod, Jubei was jog-
ging on to his house, devoid of any pleasure,
almost unconsciously as a wooden image
dragged on by a string.

"Here, fool and madcap," a harsh voice
broke upon him suddenly. "What are you going to do with my washed stuff? You idiot!"

Dumfounded at being scolded thus bitterly, Jubei looked about him, when helter-skelter came down a drying board placed against a wooden tub, on which he had been stepping unawares. He was awkwardly thrown off his feet.

"You possessed of a fox, take it!" A strong-muscled maid by the name of O-Kane, with her face round as a squash and her eyes a little out of place, gave him angrily a blow of her fist and thrust him off with her arm. Jubei rolled in the dust and unbearably:

"Yes, yes; I am possessed of a fox. So have mercy!"

Thus saying and turning deaf ears to her foul language, he ran off despite his pain, and at last reached his home.

He found his wife waiting for him. "You took much time this morning," said she; "and I was very anxious over you. But what have you done? You are soiled all over."

And she tried to dust his clothes.

"Oh, never mind." Just a word of cold refusal he dropped wearily. But seeing the kind, anxious look of his wife trying to read his face, he was dragged into the melting mood, and tears would well up in spite of him.

"Fie!" he ejaculated unwittingly as if to reproach himself, and making a ball of cut tobacco for his pipe, tried to appear calm as ever. But he was mute, and there was something unusual about him. His wife quickly guessed all, but on her part she did not know how to console him. And mortified at not being able to ask about what passed between him and the Abbot, for fear of annoying him, she was building silently a scant fire with burnt cinders by the help of a pair of hibashi not matching, one being a thrown-off chopstick, and was warming tea in a pot, when Ino, who had been out playing, came back.

"O papa, home now?" said he. "You are going to build a pagoda, aren't you? I've built one myself. Look at this."

And opening a screen cheerfully, the boy pointed at the pile with an innocent smile which anticipated a hearty approval. His mother, unable to bear the situation, gnashed her teeth and melted into silent tears, while Jubei stared at the work of his little boy with his round, swimming eyes.

"Well done, my boy; well done! You shall be rewarded for it," said he, half sobbing and half laughing, with a voice loud enough to reach his house-top. And turning his face up to heaven, he sighed:

"Ah, how hard it is to be the younger brother!"

XI

The sliding lattice-door was heard to open livelily as usual.

"O-Kichi, I am back," said Genta cheerfully as he came in.

O-Kichi, who had been spelling her anxious thoughts with the wreaths of smoke, cast her pipe aside and rose hurriedly to meet her husband.

"Quite late in coming back, aren't you?" said she, and going round to his back, helped him take off his overcoat. She then folded it quickly with the help of her chin, and laying it in a corner, came back to the fire-box. In no time she made the iron pot chirp on like a cricket, and casting a furtive glance on the face of her husband, who was squatting heavily tailor-fashion, said:

"It is sunny, but the wind is keen. You must have been cold on the way. Let me make you warm saké."

And letting her sensible service speak her heart, she set the table quickly. The lemon-spiced pickles smelled nicely, and the fresh trout's eggs served with radish sauce were simple yet toothsome.

Genta was not quite easy at heart, but being beguiled somewhat by this, took up a saké cup, and after drinking two or three cupfuls in rapid succession, drained the next one slowly.

"Have a drink, O-Kichi," said he, and handed the cup to her.

O-Kichi, after a sip, laid the cup down, and taking a piece of laver from the fire, folded it and divided it into smaller pieces.

"Sanko ought to be here pretty soon," she thought aloud of a fish-monger, and returning the cup to her husband and pouring out saké for him, said composedly with a clear voice as she felt quite sure of her husband's success:

"I wanted to ask you about your business to-day. There is no doubt of your getting the work, but until you tell me all about it, I am worried with useless anxiety. What did the Abbot say? And how about Jubei? I cannot bear to see you so grave and silent."

On this Genta laughed outright.

"Oh, don't you worry," said he. "The warm-hearted Abbot will make me any way a nice man. Ha, ha! But O-Kichi, isn't he a nice man who loves his younger brother? Under some circumstances, we have to invite the hungry to share our by no means sufficient food. I am not afraid of anybody. But to be unflinching is not all for a man. Ha, ha! He is also a man who forbears and unnerves himself in spite of him. Yes, he is a fine man, indeed. To build a pagoda is a work of honour. Would that I could leave myself a splendid monument standing for ages in the sight of thousands of men — the work finished by the hands of Genta alone, without calling into help even a particle of other men's thought or labour. But to bear the brunt is — a man. A fine man, indeed. The Abbot does not lie. It's more than I could bear to give another half of the work I have set my mind to do. Oh, how hard! But I am the elder brother. Listen, O-Kichi, I intend to give half the work to Jubei, and build the pagoda together. Am I not a fine man? Cheer me, cheer me, O-Kichi. Unless I am not cheered at least by you, I feel all too dull with the work."

And he laughed aloud an empty laugh. O-Kichi could not fathom her husband's mind.

"I don't know what the Abbot told you," she began; "but I cannot understand at all what you say. It does not sound a bit nice to me. What do you mean by giving half the work to that dull-as-a-beetle Jubei? It is not very like you. If you intend to give, you had better part with the work entirely. Of course, as you mean to get the work all to yourself, there is no use doing such an ignoble thing as to get a needless help and chop, so to speak, one man's head by two. You used to be proud of, and people gave you credit for, having a heart clean and straightforward. But what is this queer decision of yours? It appears even to me as a mere patched-up plan, born of a silly-shally mind. I cannot approve it; no, by any means. Why, the one you deal with is only that slouch who is under obligation to us., Properly speaking, he deserves our downright scolding for having intruded into our own sphere of action. And you could easily make him shut up if you would. Why need we then be so lenient with him, and enter into an irritating co-operation? It is not all merely to be lenient. And merely to be nerveless does not make you a nice man. I could not persuade myself to the contrary. But shall I, if you mind, fetch a run to Jubei's and make him feel very sorry for his ingratitude and give up all his desire?"

So O-Kichi ended her womanish remonstrance to her husband when Genta laughed her to scorn.

"I don't expect you to understand," said he. "All what you do is to think whatever I do is right."

XII

Reduced bluntly to silence with one word, O-Kichi raised her face and was about to speak something out of her unyielding disposition. But knowing from experience the uselessness of further refuting her husband more unbending than herself, if it was not, indeed, to irritate his excitable temper, she sagaciously changed her mind, though feeling ill at her husband who would not take his helpmate into his secrets.

"I should not have contradicted you," she said, "as if I had known better. But as I am thinking of your work constantly, I wanted to know so much how the matter stood, and said carelessly more than I ought to."

Thus, making light of her candid words purposely, she pretended to submit herself to the will of her husband. And this, indeed, was from her honest desire to relieve him even a little of his inner bitterness.

On this Genta softened his half-hardened countenance.

"Every thing comes by chance, you know," said he. "And if we keep ourselves meek and forbearing, another good thing may turn up. Looking from this point, I feel rather pleased to give half the work to Jubei. You will be happy or unhappy with your lot, according to your view. It seems wise to live cleanly and unselfishly, not tainting our hearts with the rust of meanness."

And he drained the cup he held in his hand. Then they shifted their talk to that of theatres and to the gossips about Genta's men, and after having had saké just enough, they ate their dinner happily together, facing across the small table.

"It's now about time for Jubei to call," thought Genta, and waited without doing anything after dinner. But time passed on vainly; the sunlight on the paper screen moved a foot, but he did not appear; it shifted two, but still he did not show up. "He ought to come by all means," Genta muttered to himself, "to talk over the matter, lowering his head and drawing in his horns, and to ask even with tears for a portion of the work on the strength of the kind words of the Abbot to-day. But how is this that he is so late in coming? Is it because he has given up all his hope and stays gloomily at home, thinking there is no further use in seeing me? Or is he waiting for me to call? If the latter be the case, I should be surprised at his conceit. But it is not probable that he should be so vain. All there is about this is perhaps no more than his usual slowness. But what a sluggard! He ought to mind his business a little bit."

So he waited, smoking away his time idly. The short winter day, which appeared long to Genta for waiting, now faded, and crows in flocks were hastening to their nightly roost, but Jubei did not come. Genta now began to feel ill at heart and could hardly suppress his blood from boiling. He merely touched his supper, and no sooner had he drunk his tea hastily than he rose with impatience.

"O-Kichi," he said in a rough voice: "I am going to Jubei's. If he happens to pass me on the way and comes in my absence, be sure to let him wait."

And he went out flushing with anger. O-Kichi, anxious as she was over her husband, could not prevent him, and after seeing him off, heaved a deep sigh.

XIII

Being irritated still more at the sliding door of Jubei's house, sticking in the groove, Genta opened it roughly by force.

"Is Jubei in?" he said and entered the house without waiting for an answer.

O-Nami, Jubei's wife, found at once by the voice who it was, and with her heart beating, felt mortified to see the guest to whom her husband owed gratitude but with whom he was now rivalling.

"Well, Genta-sama," she exclaimed before she knew, but while she was searching vainly for words of salutation for excitement, Genta passed on to a seat near Jubei who was sitting alone by the side of an old pin-holed and oil-soiled paper ando. On this O-Nami, though honest yet unused to receive a guest, asked him hurriedly to the side of the fire-box.

Jubei now bowed clumsily and opened his heavy lips.

"I was thinking of calling on you to-morrow morning."

"So, that was your intention." said Genta, casting a fiery glance on him, but purposely composed. "As for myself I waited for you from morning till evening, and as I am impatient, you know, I concluded you would never show up. Then I was foolish to be so hasty as to call on you, eh? But, Jubei, what do you think of the Abbot's words to-day? He wanted us to talk over the matter, and then told us the story of the two brothers. So I came purposely to see you about that. I think I am quite headstrong as you know, but being convinced that it boots us little to be at odds as in the fable, — and as we are by no means foes, — I shan't be utterly selfish towards you. What I want is our mutual agreement, and I have come fully prepared for it, suppressing selfish ideas and thinking out how best we can arrange the matter. But I like to get your frank opinion, and am ready to reconsider what I want to propose. I am a man, you know, and will not play false. That's what I thought honestly in coming."

He paused a while and looked at Jubei who was sitting with his head hung down. But for the occasional reply of "Yes, sir," he was mute; a few gray hairs in his unkempt locks only shone in the flickering light of the lamp. O-Nami, too, sat by the bed of her boy Inosuke, and kept silent with bated breath. The stillness of it was that the distant cry of a nightly peddler selling hot macaroni was felt faintly to creep into the house from outside.

Genta collected himself still more and continued in a calm voice:

"I shall then speak frankly of my plan first. I know why you desire this work so much.

You want to give full play to your skill, not from any idea of profit, but from that of materializing your professional ideal and leaving behind the embodiment of your design and workmanship. You may sympathize with me, for I, too, feel just like you. This is not the kind of work you come across often. If we miss this chance, perhaps we must die without it. So you see how I like to get it, too, to leave my own design and skill. To reason in my favour, I am the regular architect to the Kannoji, and you are a mere outsider; I am the first applicant, and you are the second; in fact, I was asked to submit the estimate, which I did, while you were not.

And the work itself, anybody will think, is within the bounds of my means to get a contract for, while it is beyond those of yours.

"But I shan't make an argument of them against you. I know you are unfortunate in spite of your ability, I know how much you are weeping secretly over your hard lot, though you never complain of it in public. And I know you are leading a life of sorrow, totally unbearable to me if I were in your place. So I did what best I could for you last year and the year before last, though it was nothing to speak of, and I am not speaking this to remind you specially of it. But that the Abbot should advise us like that argues his compassion towards you because of your honesty. Of course, if it were from mere money grubbing that you make a stand against me, I would not stop till I blow your brains out for thrusting audaciously your nose in another's business. But in sympathizing with you in your real situation, I'd rather give you the whole of the work. Still I cannot give up my first intention entirely. The chance is too rare to be missed.

"So, Jubei, I want you to hear me carefully. This is rather hard for me to propose, and will be equally repulsive for you to lend an ear to. But I wish you would come round by all means. Let us both build the pagoda together, with me as chief architect, and you as assistant, though you may not be well satisfied with it. Indeed, you may not be willing, but I *pray* you will give me your consent. But do you mean by your silence that you are unwilling?" Turning to Jubei's wife who was moved readily to tears, "O-Nami-san, I wish you would join me in asking your husband to comply with my request."

"I — I don't know how I can thank you, my dear sir," said she, wetting her sleeves with tears. "No one but you would make such a kind proposal." Turning to Jubei: "But why don't you thank him at all?"

O-Nami seized her husband's knees and shook him, but Jubei, dumb all this while like a stone image, still remained silent. He was urged again and again, when, lifting his face, he dropped a sentence bluntly:

"I am sorry I cannot agree to that."

O-Nami was stunned and held her breath.

"What?" ejaculated Genta sharply, and tossing his head, looked down straight at him with fire in his eyes.

XIV

That Genta should kindly make such a proposal, at once just and fair, which ordinary people would hardly do, was all out of the sincerity of his heart. And to give a point-blank refusal like Jubei, though he did so from his outspoken nature, was little less than a downright offence. Even an unfeeling waxwork would have said otherwise. And O-Nami wondered how shamelessly dim-sighted, thick-skulled her husband could be. She felt as if she were ground in a mortar in the face of Genta, and drew near to her husband impulsively.

"What do you mean by that, Jubei?" said she: "Can't you understand his exceeding kindness to let you have half the work which he would like to do all by himself? Don't you know that he is doing so, trying to be fair and feeling very sorry for our misery, while he could easily thrust us aside and have his own way if he wished? And don't you know that he does this, not by having you wait on him, but by coming himself to such a wretched place, where not even a thin cushion is provided for the guest? But confound you to answer like that with no respect for him! It is nothing but selfishness.

"But you could not pretend not to understand his kindness, could you? Then how dare you to be so insolent? Look at this dress of mine which was O-Kichi-sama's and which she gave me last year, taking pity on *my* thin clothes in cold weather. Don't you remember that? And to reject his offer altogether, without ever stopping to think of his unchanging kindness to befriend the weak as well as his generosity not to take offence at our impertinency! Even if you are utterly unwilling, can you, endowed with memory, dare to put it in that way? Think carefully whom we are facing now, and what O-Kichi-sama will think of us. How can I bear to be put out of countenance by meeting O-Kichi-sama henceforth? Genta-sama is large-minded, so he may give us up as simpletons and may not think of us any more, but what will people say about you? It's beyond doubt that they will despise you as an ungrateful, unfeeling fellow, — a crow, a dog, a beast! What honour is there to build as a crow or a dog? Don't you feel ashamed of yourself, you who used to tell me that it's foolish to be avaricious, to be too much bent on money-making?

"So, please be so gentle as to follow the advice of Genta-sama. If you share the honour with Genta-sama as one of the two who have built the towering Shoun Pagoda, all what I have suffered for you will be rewarded, and Genta-sama's unbounded kindness will be made known thereby. Oh, how happy I shall be then! I believe I shall not be able to find even a shadow of discontentment anywhere; but what evil spirit makes you think otherwise? O bless my heart! That you should forget yourself thus!"

In tears O-Nami remonstrated. And a thread, which was drooping over her lowered head, from the needle stuck on her knotted hair, trembled as her heart swelled with emotions, when Jubei, who had remained with his eyes closed, opened his mouth.

"Shut up, O-Nami," said he, in his usual coarse voice. "You are too clamorous. You disturb our talk. — Genta-sama, listen to me, if you please."

XV

Jubei, gathering his knees shaking with emotion, and holding them fast with his hands, said:

"You don't know, Genta-sama, how I feel to be asked to do the work by both together. It looks very kind of you to give me half the work, but really you are unfeeling. I don't like to do that. To build a pagoda is my burning desire, but I have already given this up. On my way home from the temple this morning, I made up my mind to forgo it. It was a great mistake for me to cherish the idea beyond my reach. Indeed, I was too foolish. It's the part of the slouch to be always a dullard and a fool. I shall live and die content with mending gutters. You will pardon me, Genta-sama; I was wrong; I shan't say any more that I like to build the pagoda. You are no stranger to me but a kind patronizer, and I shall watch, and feel happy to see, you build a splendid pagoda alone."

Hardly had Jubei's cheerless words been finished when the impetuous Genta, as if unable to hear him through, drew nearer.

"You talk nonsense, Jubei," he said. "You are too unreasonable. The Abbot's advice was not for you alone, but for me as well. While it went into your head, it also sank in my breast. If you disappear, as it were, into the depths, carrying all the burden on you alone, Genta will have no chance to be a man. No one would praise your too modest idea to withdraw yourself for paltry reasons and to remain content with being a fool, as a wise plan. To take the work upon myself straightway, by way of taking time by the forelock, would be disgraceful in the face of the Abbot. And then the principle of honour, which I closely followed so far, would not avail me anything, and, of course, you would gain nothing thereby. What good then would it bring to either of us? So I say we will do the work both together beautifully. You may find it somewhat not to your liking, but that is mutual, and so far as you are not satisfied, you must know that I don't feel quite at home myself either. But there is no reason why we cannot make concession each other. And, indeed, you need not persuade yourself purposely and with difficulty that you are a fool, scatter to the winds your pains of many days, and bury away your splendid workmanship. So, Jubei, if you understand what I say, do change your mind entirely. I don't say anything unreasonable. But why do you remain silent? Are you still dissatisfied? Can't you give me your consent? Or are you still unable to see my point? Come, Jubei, what is the matter with you? You ought to answer me anyway. It will never do to be dumb like an animal. Do you think I am not reasonable? Or did you get sulky by my words?"

Thus Genta, as a true Yedonian who was strong in honour as well as in kindness, asked Jubei gently. O-Nami, listening to him, was thrilled with gratitude, and though she was speechless, her tears were eloquent. Feeling uneasy for her husband, she cast her dim eyes toward him when she saw Jubei remaining rigid as a stone, hanging his head heavily in mute silence, and shedding tears, whose drops seemed to strike his knees with a sound. Even Genta was now wordless and was musing for a while.

"Jubei, you don't understand me yet, do you?" he broke silence at last. "Or are you really dissatisfied? You feel disappointing, I suppose, to do by two of us the work you set your mind on to start alone. And then you feel bitterer to do it with me as chief and you as assistant? Well now," — Genta quickly making up his mind to suppress his desire in spite of himself — "let me concede further. I don't care to be the assistant, so you will be the chief. How do you like it? Give me your cheerful consent to what I propose."

"Heaven forbid!" cried Jubei. "Though I lose my mind, how can I dare to do that? It's monstrous."

"Then do you take my first offer?" Genta pressed.

"That —," Jubei stammered.

"Then we will make you as chief. But are you still dissatisfied?"

Being pressed too hard, Jubei lost himself. His wife, seeing this, was all in a flutter.

"Why don't you follow his advice quickly?" O-Nami urged half reproachfully and half pleadingly. Jubei, now driven to the last extremity, had only to speak but his mind frankly, and raising his head and rolling his large eyes, said:

"Chief or assistant, I cannot do one piece of work in co-operation with another; simply because I don't like it. You may build the pagoda by yourself. I shall remain a fool." Genta was offended, and without waiting for him to finish his words, exclaimed:

"Even defying my endeavour thus to try and meet you half-way?"

"Yes; I thank you for your kindness, but I do not lie. I cannot do it because I don't like it."

"That's boldly spoken. But you cannot on any account reconsider my words?"

"That's more than I could do."

"You dull-head, you dog," thundered Genta; "you insensible to human feeling! How dare you? Take the consequences then! I will not speak to you any more. Lead the life of drudgery! I will not let you even touch the pagoda. It shall be built splendidly by Genta alone. Find fault, if you can, with my work!"

XVI

"No, thank you. I get drunk. I cannot take any more," said Seikichi as he bowed many times, but as usual with a merry, self-contradicting saké-bibber, he still allowed his cup being filled as it was emptied. He had, indeed, been treated to saké, but still retaining a touch of soberness for his reserve, sat up straight.

"It won't do," he continued; "to be flushed like this in our master's absence. I must be careful not to get too merry and begin dancing at this early hour of the evening, having you as my fair drinking mate. Ha, ha! I don't know why, but I feel very light of heart. I shall be going, however; if I exceed the bounds of propriety, I shall be scolded by our master. But, ma'am, I like him even if he reads me a lecture. I don't mean to say anything unkind, but between you and me, I really feel more grateful to your husband than my chabukuro (tea bag). While we were working at the Ryounin, I happened to fall out with Tetsu and Kei from a trivial cause, and gave a deep cut at the shoulder of Tetsu. His mother then came to my house, and in tears complained of her misery. I repented of my deed and felt very sorry for her. But we were very poor, too, and could not do anything for them. I was so much troubled that I almost made up my mind to run away from the spot, when our master silently sent necessary aid to Tetsu. And without giving me a bit of hard words, he said mildly:

"'Now, Sei, you may not help quarreling under some circumstances; but if you feel sorry for that fellow, you had better apologize to him. His mother will feel reconciled to, and your peace at night will be all the calmer.'

"I did not know what to think of his kind-heartedness, and only wept for it. I had no reason to apologize to Tetsu, but for the sake of my master, I went to do so. After that, strange enough, Tetsu and I were good friends before we knew, and now we are so devoted to each other that, in case one come to an untimely end, the other vows to collect his ashes. And all this through the kind act of our master. My chabukuro, on the contrary does nothing but to find fault with me. She pesters me with lectures not to quarrel, not to fool my time away, and about a hundred other trivial nots. Ha, ha, indeed, you would hardly believe me. Who is chabukuro? Why, it is my ofukuro (mother). No, I am not bad to call her so; she deserves it. And it is not an ordinary kind of fukuro (bag), but one used for the inferior kind of tea and painted with an astringent solution, you know. Aha, ha! I thank you very much for your entertainment. I must be going now. Why, another bottle? Do you say

I must have it, too, because you warmed the saké? I don't know how I can thank you. If I were drinking at home, my chabukuro, unlike you, would insist to lay aside my cup before I had the last bottle. But I never felt so cheerful as now. I feel like singing. Can I sing, do you say? Gracious, you ask me such a question. My 'matsuzukushi' has been encored by *her.*"

"As if to wind up with your sweetheart!" laughed O-Kichi.

At this moment Genta came back, and seeing Seikichi, said:

"Well now, Seikichi. This is lucky: let's drink. O-Kichi, get something more. Seikichi, drink like a fish this evening, and we will hear you bellow 'matsuzukushi.'"

Seikichi, surprised:

"Well, you overheard us, didn't you?"

XVII

As he got drunk, Seikichi lost his constraint, and on account of the familiar way in which Genta and his wife treated him, he soon forgot his reserve. And without refusing as many more cupfuls as he was offered, he drank deep, and brightening his lovely red cheeks still more, like ripe winter-cherries, laughed an innocent horse laugh, or gave himself airs against a shadow. He then gossiped about this fellow or that, boasted himself on being once cheered for his success in imitating a certain actor's voice, and told about his knocking down a night-watch in a temple compound, and about a very comical failure of his friend Sen, after disputing with him the practicability of the joke, to steal a large bronze firebox from some teahouse. And as he was thus chattering on one thing after another as it was suggested, the talk happened to drift on that of Jubei, when he, staring with his bedimmed eyes, shrugging his relaxed shoulders, and draining his half emptied cup with a queer twist in his lips, said:

"I cannot understand at all why you favour such a fool as he. At work he is only overcareful and is everlastingly slow. In planing a pillar or a lintel, he would whet his tool three times. There is nothing that he could finish in time.

Sen used to laugh at Jubei as being a sort of fellow who took three days for making red pine frame for a small fire-place, but that is true. But as you looked kindly on such a fellow, Kin, Sen, Roku, and I did not feel very well for a while — excuse my frankness — at your magnanimity, and thought perversely that if over-carefulness alone would win your favour, we would give a nice polish even to weather boards, and do the work slowly. But you know he is also such an unsociable, blunt fellow who would never visit a tea-house or have a drink with us over a hot chicken pot-pourri. When we went to the Daishi Shrine together, we thought we might not leave any one uninvited, who worked under you, and so I called on him kindly for that purpose. What do you think he told me? He only said that he was too poor to go. What a blunt, cold answer to one's kindness! Though he had no money, he should, as a friend, try to bear company with us, even going so far as to pawn the only change of his wife. Indeed, though fool, he may now be said independent like Kin and me, all through your kind support, but unlike us who apprenticed you from snotty-nosed boyhood, carrying at first lunch boxes to the work-shed in the morning, and in the evening carrying home bunches of chips, — unlike us, Jubei was, so to speak, a migrant, a wanderer. Properly speaking, he should feel more grateful to you than most of us, but Genta-sama — O-Kichi-sama — I feel like crying. If something should happen to you, I don't hesitate to go through smoke and fire for your sake. But you dog, you unfeeling fellow, you slouch, you will not dare to do the feat, though heapt with boundless favour! You inferior even to beasts!"

So sobbed Seikichi, turning endlessly his discontent in his giddy mind. O-Kichi, being troubled at his usual trick, looked at her husband's face, but remained silent, finding Seikichi's word somewhat close to her heart because of her hatred of Jubei. Genta, however, was not foolish enough to be carried away by such an appeal, and offering his saké cup to Seikichi, laughed aloud:

"What are you talking about?" said he. "Remember where you are. No use crying like that. To be sure, you might win a woman's heart in that way. But this is not the room of your Kocho-sama you took pride to speak of."

Seikichi got all the more earnest for such a jest, and clearing his eyes of large beads of tears with his hand, and thrusting it unceremoniously into a fish plate, cried out convulsively:

"Ah me! you don't know me, master. You treat me as one intoxicated. But I am not drunk. I have not eaten Kocho. But why does her face appear to me somewhat like that of Jubei? It breaks my heart to think of it. Indeed, no one is more hateful to me than the slouch, who is so conceited as to try to build such a big thing as a pagoda, even thrusting you aside. He is a rebel flying in the face of our too merciful master. A rebel like Akechi has reason for his act, so I heard a story-teller say. But when did you strike Jubei's head with your iron-ribbed fan as Nobunaga did? When did you tell him that you were going to deprive him of his estate and give it to Ranmaru? Such a despicable traitor as Jubei will never be found. If he, emboldened by your kind word, is so arrogant as to build the pagoda jointly with you, I shall not be a mere looker-on. I will blow his brains out, and cast his flesh to dogs. Yes, I will — even like this."

And with his fist Seikichi knocked an empty bottle hard; it scattered in broken fragments and sent small dishes flying.

"You fool!" roared Genta, when Seikichi sat down crushingly and was seen remaining silent, with his brow low on the scattered bits of dried laver. He was snoring already.

"An amiable fool!" laughed Genta. "Cover him warm."

And then he drank some more by himself, and breathing a long hot breath a moment, paused to say:

"I came back offended, but to stop short right here would make me not very much different from Seikichi. I have to think deeper still."

XVIII

After Genta had gone provoked, Jubei was sitting with folded arms, bewildered. O-Nami looked in his face and heaved a sigh.

"You've offended Genta-sama," she thoughtfully observed: "and you've lost your work, too. Not only you throw to the dogs all your labour and pains of many nights in making that model, but you hurt people's feelings and will be known shamelessly as ungrateful and insensible. What a pity! You might reject my words as ill-advised because of a woman's, but you are too simple-minded to be wise. It would be none of your shame to follow Genta-sama's kind advice and to do the work jointly. No one will praise you for your stubbornness. On the contrary, you will give Genta-sama, much delight, as you know, to do as he desired, and then you could make your name and be rewarded for your pains. Why, you will be all right on every side, but how is this that you can't turn your thought in that way? I cannot understand you at all. Can you not think over and change your mind to take his advice? If you do so, I will go at once to Genta-sama's and implore his pardon in some way. Yes, I will not move, though I may be struck and kicked, till I gain my object. If I beg and beg his pardon a thousand times, Genta-sama, kind at heart, will not long remain offended. He will surely forgive and forget your obstinacy. Then won't you let me do it?"

"Don't speak any more about that," said Jubei, who listened to the sensible advice of his wife, even without moving his eyes. "Don't speak any more about that. Oh, don't mention even the name of pagoda. I may be called ungrateful and insensible because I cherished such an extravagant desire. But I cannot help it now; all has come from my shallow judgment. But I hate to change my mind for the world as you want me to. In my work I may engage carpenters, but I don't want any advisers. I may be employed as a mere hand in others' work, but I shan't intrude on their work by giving my own idea. In adjusting overlapping corners or in arranging rafters, I will do it in my own style and will not be directed by any man. For better or for worse, I shoulder the responsibility by myself. When engaged in others' work, I shall do honestly just so much as I am ordered to, and shall not be so conceited as to offer any presumptuous opinion. I dislike those parasites who take pride in what little contribution they make as if it were all, while they are mere tools in another's hand. As I hate to be parasitic on another's work, so I hate to have anyone parasitic on my work, too.

There is no help for it. I perfectly understand and thank for what Genta-sama, trying to be fair and kind, was good enough to suggest. But it's a pity that he should treat me parasitically. I don't trouble myself to be called slow or foolish. But I don't care for being parasitic and prosperous. I may wither away like a weed or be a fertilizer to a big tree, But you know, as often as I saw a fellow who became a parasite and perched high, I used to despise him as mean and low-minded: can I then unblushingly become one now, induced even by the kindness of Genta-sama? I should rather be employed by Genta-sama and follow his instructions to plane this and to saw that. But, indeed, his kindness is my grief. You may perhaps feel bad at my doggedness, but be forbearing. Ah, but there is no help for it. Doggedness is what I am. People call me, on that account, slouch, fool, or idiot, but let them say so. Why, charcoal has burned down, and it's getting colder. We'd better go to bed now, O-Nami."

O-Nami, listening attentively to her husband's reasonable view, had no word to say against him, and remained silent, when the flickering flame of the ando, lighting the cold room, dimmed with the charred wick.

XIX

That night Genta could not sleep very well. Hearing quite distinctly the first and the second crowing of a cock, he rose earlier than usual, and washed his vague dreams away, and with a cup of hot fragrant tea, cleared the lingering smell of saké, when Seikichi got up, and rubbing his sleepy eyes, stood bewildered, as one who did not know where he was. At last Genta burst out with his wife and teased him:

"Where were you last night, Seikichi?"

Being reminded, Seikichi sat suddenly in a respectable way, and bowing many times, apologized:

"I went to sleep before I knew, being treated to too much saké. But didn't I do anything rude last night?"

"Oh, never mind," said O-Kichi. "Get ready for your breakfast now, and go to your work before late."

Seikichi, however feared worse for her gentle words, and being honest, behaved humbled.

After Seikichi was gone, Genta was busied in his thought, and far from being cheerful, did not even talk to his wife. He was heard to think aloud, "Now I have it!" and then to sigh, "What a pity!" "Shall I give it up?" he muttered after a while; "Damn!" — he seemed to take offence at something. O-Kichi, unable to watch her husband idly, tried to ease his disquiet by sharing his mind, but being put to silence ruthlessly, was only worrying in her bosom. Genta, not caring a bit for such things, pondered over and over in his mind till toward evening, and making up his mind at last, rose to change his dress.

He went straightway to the Kannoji, and seeing the Abbot, told him frankly all that happened the night before.

"I came back offended at the too unreasonable reply of Jubei," he went on, "and determined to build the pagoda alone. But as I thought it over and over, I found that however splendidly I might build it, I could not thereby show how I was benefited by your kind advice, but, on the contrary, I should be known only as a self-centred, ignoble fellow. But Jubei will not for the world change his mind. As he, however, suppressed his own desire and gave the whole work to me, I must do the same on my part with my wish, and try to cede, asking the work be handed over to him. It can't be helped that Jubei won't agree to what I thought the best plan in my shallow mind; there is, indeed, no use in resenting that. But as I cannot think out another good plan, I come to you, Abbot, asking to be commanded. Give your order, then, to Jubei or to me or to both together just as you please. We will not object to anything if it comes from you. We could not decide the matter between us alone."

The Abbot smiled pleasantly at Genta's sincere looks.

"Well, I am glad you came to see me," said he. "I thought you would. And I feel proud of you thinking like that. You are, indeed, a man as I expected. You are ennobled by that intention of yours alone more than you would by building a splendid pagoda. You may not know, but Jubei was here also before you and went away, saying just the same thing. Isn't he a good fellow? Now, Genta, you will befriend him, will you?"

"Yes, surely I will, "answered Genta. cheerfully, guessing hastily at what the Abbot appeared to hint at.

"Very good," said the Abbot, his face all wrinkled with smile. "Oh, what a pleasant fellow you are!"

Being lauded from the bottom of the Abbot's hearts, Genta was overjoyed and looked up involuntarily from his reverential attitude.

"Thank heaven, I am now a man," he said and wept from the fullness of his heart. He now formed a beautiful resolution to do what he could for Jubei's success.

XX

The day was a sad one to Jubei, when he went to the Kannoji and told the Abbot, with tears, of his intention of giving up the work. As he returned home, he was so dispirited that he felt powerless even to think of taking up his pipe. And as he blankly reflected on his unfortunate lot and the miserable life he led, he was all the more depressed. The meal he ate was all the same, but his hand holding the sticks moved only slowly, and his appetite almost deserted him. He took only one or two bowls of rice, though in the habit of devouring six or seven bowls, and as usual with one whose mind was burdened, he was sipping altogether too much tea. As Jubei was spiritless, his wife and even his innocent but wayward boy, Ino, looked depressed, and the lonesome hut appeared all the more so. They spent the day without a smile and passed the night, dreaming cheerless dreams. O-Nami, awakened by the bell of the dawn, cautiously slipped out of bed, where she slept with Ino, wanting to leave him there undisturbed till she made a fire, for the morning was cold. But without sleeping on as usual, unconscious of every thing, he jumped out of bed at once; apparently from no cause, and tumbling on it, cried out with his tiny hands over his eyes:

"Help, help my pa! He is knocked!"

"What is the matter, Ino?" Surprised, O-Nami took him in her arms, but he did not stop crying.

"You are dreaming, Ino. Nothing happens to your pa. See, he is sleeping there still." And she turned his face toward Jubei.

The boy peeped at his father puzzlingly. He felt somewhat reconciled but was still in doubt.

"Nothing strange here; see, Ino. You are frightened by your dream. Come, don't catch cold. You must be in bed. It's still early." And O-Nami pushed him into bed, and covering him with a comforter, patted him.

"I was frightened," said the boy, his eyes wide open. "A bad man —"

"Well, what did he do?"

"With a big, big hammer, he struck papa's head. He struck again and again till pa's head got half smashed. I did not know how frightened I was."

"For heaven's sake, don't tell me such a terrible thing." And O-Nami drew her brows together when she happened to hear outside the bean-vender, familiar to her for his tremulous voice, was muttering, "Damn! Such a bad luck with my sandal!"

Feeling still more ill at ease, she went to the kitchen. But the fire-wood in the range would burn only poorly, and the sliding window in the roof would creak irritably in opening. She knew that the day appeared only dismal because of her mind, but curious enough, she met many evidences of its really being so, being perhaps all too much concerned about them. Thinking, however, she would be laughed at if she spoke of them, she rebuked herself, and with spirit in her words, and smiling more cheerfully than usual, she attended on her husband and looked after her boy; but as it was all feigned, her laughter died off sad and hollow, and made the world all the gloomier for that.

Just then a voice haughty and affected was heard outside:

"Is Jubei in?" And a boy bonz from the Kannoji came in and sat down, giving airs to his little person. "You are wanted at once at the temple."

Jubei as well as O-Nami could not understand at all the purport of this curt message, but as he could not afford to neglect the call, he made haste to go with the boy, though thinking it almost useless to cross the gate of the Kannoji. As he, however, reported himself at the office, he was shown to a room where he found, heavens and earth! the Abbot, with Yendo, the Head Monk, on his right, and Tameyemon, the Secretary, on his left, awaiting him!

It was Yendo who spoke gravely:

"Jubei, the building of the Shoun Pagoda, which was to be entrusted to Genta Kawagoye, will, through a special favour and consideration of the Abbot, be entrusted wholly to you. This is not to be refused. Your ready consent is expected."

This delivered, the Abbot added in his husky voice:

"Now, Jubei, put your very best into the work. I shall be delighted with your success." Jubei, who had been thunderstruck at this unexpected turn, bowed suddenly flat at the gracious word of the Abbot, and writhing under the swelling emotions, stammered:

"I shall st — stake my life —"

Tears choked him, and in the still, spacious chamber, only his sobbing wove tremulous waves.

XXI

Sweet summer with the fragrance of pink and white lotus-flowers, wafted over the lake, with the beads of dew trembling on the floating leaves, and with the morning breeze wandering among old nodding stalks, was gone long before, and now the dragon-flies began to disport with water-caltrops, and the early frost tinged yonder leafy hills. But the solitary heron, wading slowly among the reddened stalks, now leafless and sad-looking, was lovely to see, while the evening sky deepening in dark blue, with faintly shining stars and with some wild geese flying across it and crying soft, plaintive cries, was all the heart could desire.

In a room on the second story of the teahouse, Horaiya, overlooking this beautiful scene of Shinobazu Pond, sat a pleasant-looking man waiting for someone. He was neatly dressed in plain cotton, and carried an unpretentious silver pipe of Sumiyoshi make, which bespoke of his genteel nature, in spite of his workman-like mannerism. He was Genta.

Presently a woman of the house by the name of O-Den, well known to bosses like Genta, came in, carrying a small table. She set it before him as she said:

"She keeps you waiting long, doesn't she?"

Genta, just to beguile the time:

"Well, this is more than I could bear. What is she doing, I wonder, regardless of my waiting?"

"But she is not to blame to take time in dressing," she retorted, laughing.

"You are right. Look at her well when she comes. Perhaps you will find her next to none in this neighbourhood."

"You don't say so! But what do you treat me to for listening to your boasting? And is she a teacher in dancing?"

"Oh, no."

"An ordinary miss?"

"Far from it."

"A widow?"

"None of that."

"An old woman?"

"You joke. How on earth —"

"Then I have it. A baby!"

"Now stop fooling."

Genta laughed, and the woman, too, when another maid was heard to call outside the screen.

"O-Den-san, your service —"

Some one had come. O-Den rose to attend the door, but turning round a bit and looking purposely into Genta's eyes, smiled without a word. She was perhaps taking pleasure in teasing and irritating him, as she thought, by reading his mind, but without knowing that she was being laughed at secretly by Genta, she opened the door, when who should have entered but a clumsy-looking fellow, quite another thing from a fair woman! Unshaved and unkempt, the man was in rags and dirty all over. O-Den was thunderstruck at his repulsive appearance, and could not easily say a word of salutation. Genta smiled and said:

"Hello, Jubei. Come right here. No need of ceremony; make yourself quite at home."

Jubei, reserved as he was, was made to sit opposite Genta, and after a new table was set before him, Genta drained the newly filled cup of saké, and offered it to his companion.

"Jubei," said Genta, "I sent Tomimatsu this afternoon to fetch you here, because I wanted to make matters up with you, — to make clean our breasts over saké, and to have you forget all my rudeness I did the other night. Now listen; it is like this. The other night I thought you were an obstinate, unreasonable fellow, and, shameful to say, I was offended at you, and wanted very much to knock you on the head. But luckily I was not completely possessed by the devil, and on hearing at home what nonsense Seikichi said, I thought how shamelessly a narrow-minded fellow would say foolish things as if he were reasonable. I felt tickled to hear him, but just that moment I remembered what I said at your house that evening. It wasn't very different from his. I blushed at that and felt sorry that I had been carried away foolishly in my anger. My honour would be tainted, I thought, if I acted perversely, irritated at your resigning everything. That was a great mistake, and I should be disgraced in the eyes of the Abbot if I left the matter so.

"But still I felt hurt at your over-obstinacy, and found it very hard to suppress my rankling, having what I had thought out with a heart not altogether selfish, rejected point-blank. But again I thought and thought the matter carefully from one end to the other, and having made up my mind at last, I went to see the Abbot. A word of approval, however, he said when he heard me through, cleared away at once the mist in my mind, and made me feel refreshing as the cool breeze in the serene sky.

"Yesterday I went again to see the Abbot on his special invitation, when after commending me much, he told me that the work was all entrusted to you, and so wished me to be of help to you in secret. 'By this,' he said, 'you will sow the seed of happiness and prosperity. I don't think that Jubei keeps any workmen under him. So when he starts his work, he has to engage a good many of them, and, no doubt, among them some of your men will be included. You had better tell them not to be unruly or quarrelsome.' Such was the Abbot's thoughtful advice, and I came back humbled for his far-reaching kindness. But Jubei, you will pardon my rashness the other night, will you? If you now understand me thoroughly, I trust you will keep company with me as warmly as ever. As we come to know each other, to think further on what we said or did, would be as useless as to recount our dreams. And as it may do harm, and certainly do no good, to keep them in our head, let us cast them into the water of Shinobazu Pond, and forget them all.

"In buying timbers and in engaging coolies, you will meet not a little difficulty if you are not well known. So I will lend you my name and my hands as well. Those big lumbering firms, like Marucho, Yamaroku, Yenshuya, will not easily trust you if you are not a regular customer, so you make free use of me so that you may have nothing unsatisfactory. Eiji, the boss of Me Division, is a quick fellow, as you know, but as he is taking pride that his bones are of iron, and his spirit, a fire-ball, if you trust him completely, he will never shrink from his duty. Nothing is more important in building a pagoda than to harden the foundation ground so as to resist the effect of elements. And if you let Fire-ball Eiji do it, he will vow to make it firmer, if he has nothing but his spirit, than the rock on which the immovable god Fudo is seated. I will introduce you to him by and by. My sole desire at this moment is to see you successfully build the pagoda. I have no other pleasure than that. Don't you feel sorry if anything disagreeable should spoil the thing which will remain hundreds of years hence and be seen by our posterity? If they laugh and say that in the days of Genta and Jubei, people quarreled over such a miserable building, do you think our spirits can find their rest? To be an unskilled workman and to make no attempt at publicity, would not be very much of disgrace, but to be ridiculed by one's posterity for what one leaves behind, would be like a foolish father being reproved by his son, and much more shameful than a son lectured by his father. To be crucified alive would be far better than to be crucified dead and after being cured by salting.

"I did not think so deeply at first, but as I found you rivalling me, and that resolutely, I was worked up to such a pitch of determination that in workmanship I should not be surpassed by anybody. But the fire thus struck enabled me to see things more and more deeply and truly till, strange enough, my selfish will has been purged away, and nothing is now left of me but the heart to rejoice at your success and to feel your honour as mine, too. This is what I wanted to say this evening. Why, Jubei, you've heard me, moistening your big eyes! How glad I am!"

Listening immovably to Genta, who, as a true Yedonian that combined the two opposite traits of kindness and quick-temperedness in one and had no middle, was strong in the one as fierce in the other, Jubei clinched at the matting.

"Genta-sama," he said "excuse me; I don't know how to say. But I—I thank you for your kindness."

And he bowed flat, and foolishly yet honestly shed his tears.

XXII

Genta was overjoyed at this all too brief yet sincere expression of Jubei's gratitude, and looking mild and happy as a hazy morn in spring, spoke again fluently.

"As we get familiar again like this, and have nothing disagreeable left between us, we may be said to have done according to the Abbot's wish, and that creditably to both of us. Well, any way I never felt so happy as this. Come, Jubei, have enough of saké. I'll drink to my heart's content, too." Rising he took down a package from the shelf, and discovered two bundles of paper from it.

"Jubei," he continued, "have a look at this. One of them is the minute estimates, which I made out, after many nights' work, on the material, labour, and every other item of expenditure in building the pagoda. The other is all the plans of the building and its parts, most of which I specially designed myself. Some of them have been handed down from our ancestors as treasure, the plans which I cannot make public; and some are copies of the famous pagodas at Kyoto, Nara, and other places. Now, as I don't need them now, I will leave all with you. If you care to look through them, you may find something of help to you."

Jubei listened through and was not insensible to Genta's broad-mindedness to give away ungrudgingly what he put his own soul in. But he had his own way, and did not like to build his fame with others' stones.

"Genta-sama," he said, "I thank you very much. But I appreciate your kindness all the same if I don't avail myself of it. Please withdraw all this."

Genta was not pleased at this answer, too bluntly spoken, if not so intended.

"You don't say you have no need of this, do you?" he asked, concealing his sullenness.

"Yes, I am sorry I can't —," Jubei replied carelessly; unable to read his companion's mind aright.

The quick-tempered Genta could not bear any longer, and without waiting for Jubei to finish his words, said:

"Look here, Jubei. This is unexpected of you that you should push back rudely what my utmost kindness prompted me to offer. Is it because you are too proud of your skill that you slight others' suggestion? Have you forgotten that you were left to do what you like only because out of pity I forbore in anger when I found you rivalling me, while there was every reason to do anything I desired with you for your audacity? Are you still ignorant of all my struggle to suppress my bitterness when you rejected my offer selfishly, which I thought out to the best of my ability, in accordance with the wish of the Abbot, and which I made to you, taking the trouble to call on you myself? Do you think it was merely because of your good fortune that you've come to be entrusted with the work? Or is it merely your workmanship and honesty that induced the Abbot to do so? Do you think I do this that I may put you under obligation? Or have you got already so conceited as to despise others' plans as altogether worthless? Well, I don't press you hard if you don't care for them. But you are a very narrow-minded, unfeeling fellow. It is but becoming for anybody in your situation to welcome such suggestions, and adopting one or two good points, to feel grateful for the beautiful effects they have produced. But you do not so much as try to glance over them and dare to set them aside scornfully as if you know them all! Are my plans nothing more than what you are familiar with? Don't my designs go beyond the range of your invention? Absurd! But if you feel no need of seeing mine, I know what you can do. Just an ordinary thing you will build I can see now before me. I am prepared, I am sorry to say, to find fault with it. Well, this puts an end to all. I am relentless. I shan't wreak my anger meanly, but when time comes, I will surely take my fierce revenge on you. I have talked much till I get hoarse, but I shan't speak any more. I have given up the matter and shall not come cowardly to talk again with you. However long it may be — five years or ten years — I will wait in the shade, staring at you dumb, with my fiery eyes, till I get a good chance to avenge myself." Lowering his voice and addressing Jubei purposely with a polite formal title, "Now, Jubei-dono, I shall put these papers away if I can't interest you. The pagoda you will build alone, must be a splendid thing. It will never be shaken down by an earthquake or by a blast of wind, eh?"

Jubei, divining the sarcasm, was not pleased.

"I know what a shame is, slow as I am," he said rather proudly.

"That's well said. Take care lest you should forget it," said Genta, looking at him angrily. After a pause he suddenly rose. "Why, I have forgotten an important business. Jubei-dono, you stay here as long as you like. I must go back at once."

And Genta slipped out of the room as a wind in no time, amidst the surprising looks of all, left some money to cover the probable charges as he guessed, and went away.

He, however, went immediately to another tea-house on the same street, and no sooner was he in than he exclaimed:

"Damn all this foolishness! How provoking! Enough to drive me mad! — Heigh, waitress, bring saké at once. What are you taking time about? Are you going to serve me with these candles? Haven't you anything better than all this dullness? Go and fetch me girls quick — Kokane, Harukichi, O-Fusa, Choko. Don't let any one of them excuse herself. And you boys, go to my house and tell Sei, Sen, Tetsu, Masa, and everybody to come here at once."

He drank the while he said this, and as the girls came in, he surprised them right away with his impetuous words: "Away with those spiritless good evenings. But drink first; pour saké like a waterfall. Send round your cups and never have them idle. Hey, O-Fusa, stop feigning such modesty. O-Haru, did you get too old to be merry? And O-Cho, is your blood circulating? Shall I wake you up by setting off fire-crackers on your head? Come, let's have songs. Play on your samisen. Kokane, you have a good voice. Oh, that's the way; dance on. Jump higher, you wench." Turning to the newcomers, "Well, Seikichi and Tetsu, make merry this evening. I have good cause to rejoice. Mind nobody and run riot."

As the master was in extremely high spirits, his men, including Sen and Masa, who joined later, were carried away by the excitement, and they jumped about and roared, not caring if the floor gave way or the ceiling came down. They shouted and cheered at the jingles of 'Itakodejima' or 'Jinku', slipped and tumbled in dancing to the tune of 'Kappore.' Now Tetsu made a drum of a waterbasin to some jangling performance while Seikichi lay down by the side of O-Fusa, hammering catches with her silver hairpin, and Masa, wanting something extraordinary, shrieked out an offhand jargon: "Northward the ragged green hill crouched." And as the game of ken played by hands got more and more riotous, Genta cried:

"Now stop. Let's quit."

And the men followed Genta out of the house, and went where his crazy fancy carried him to.

XXIII

When a hawk catches a bird, it flies straight
as an arrow, and defying the wind and pierc-
ing the clouds, it never desists from the pur-
suit till it claws the throat of its prey. So it
was with Jubei. Since he was ordered to build
the pagoda at last, he had set his whole soul
on the work, awake or asleep; in breaking his
fast, he was chewing the tower in his mind;
in dreaming on his pillow, his soul was cir-
cling round the spire. And naturally, while
at work, he forgot all about his wife and
son; he never thought of his yesterday nor
did he dream of his to-morrow. But when he
lifted his adz to dress timbers, he put all his
strength in the sweep; when he drew a plan,
he poured his utmost into every line. To be
sure, the five feet of his body moved in the
world where cocks crowed and dogs barked,
and where the sad and the joyful were mingled together, but his soul was unfettered by
any worldly care, and was strenuously bent
on his work. Of course, at first he felt sorry
that he hurt Genta's feelings at the Horaiya,
but as his natural carelessness got better of
him, he thought slightly of it as if it were the
wind that blows ill to nobody, and then un-
feelingly enough, dropt it entirely out of his
mind, and worked on doggedly like a foolish

old cow which knows no other way but the one she is wont to tread.

The rite being successfully performed to the gods and goddess, Otsuchimioya-no-Kami, Haniyamahiko-no-Kami, Haniyama-himeno-Kami, and other gods of the soil, by offering each the five kinds or sacred metals and stones, incense, medicine, and cereal, the ground was marked, and the earth was dug. And the foundation was laid; beginning from the auspicious corner of the month, and proceeding from left to right, and finishing the work by honouring the five stars of fortune. Then the opening rites for the use of tools were solemnized by paying homage to the seven deities, Amanohitotsu-no-Mikoto, the discoverer of the art of forging, Teokihoöi-no-Mikoto, Hikosachi-no-Mikoto, Omoikane-no-Mikoto, Amatsukoyane-no-Mikoto, and Futodama-no-Mikoto, all the first architects, and Kukunochi-no-Kami, the god of timbers. Next was the ceremony of the four pillars, representing the Pillars of four Heavens, Taitoradaji-Tenno in the east, Biroshakumoku-Tenno in the west, Bishamontamon-Tenno in the north, and Biruroshazocho-Tenno in the south. Eternal protection was called upon the three starry goddesses of Tensei, Shikisei, and Tagwan, and upon the seven stars of the Dipper, and the officiating priest tightened the wedges in the joints of the pillars, by striking each three times in turn, praying that the building would stand secure for a thousand, nay, a million years.

The thing which cost Jubei a good deal of pains and labour, progressing thus successfully, he was filled with delight till even his dirty face became radiant And as they chanted at the last ceremony the old song beginning with —

"The pillars of rock immovably rooted,"

he felt happy from the bottom of his heart, and as they closed it with —

"So man's fame is built immovable and firm,"

he could not help repeating the line smilingly. Most reverently he bowed at the altar and prayed for the ultimate success by twice clapping his hands piously.

Things were totally different at the house of Genta. It was all dull and gloomy, Genta was strong-willed and did not show his feeling, but his wife, though trying to make the best of the situation, could not help feeling cross as she heard people say that on the day previous the marking of the ground for the pagoda at the Kannoji had been done, or that that day the ceremony of the pillars had been performed. "What an ungrateful fellow Jubei is!" she would say. "Is he going to make his name at the expense of my husband's broad-mindedness? But even if he is, ought he not to come to thank for our kindness for what he has already achieved? But does he remain elated, forgetting all this? If my husband is too good-natured, Jubei is provokingly insensible." And she fretted and chafed, tore her guiltless hair as it fell over her brow, and fulminated against a poor beggar who happened to come to the door.

One day, when Genta was away, a talkative physician with a shaved head, well known to the family, came to visit, and while gossiping on all sorts of things, told O-Kichi what he had heard from O-Den of the teahouse, Horaiya, where he chanced to drop in one evening. As he expressed his admiration for Genta, by way of flattering the hostess, O-Kichi did not lose a moment to gather from him all the information he could supply. And this added fuel to the flame; she first hated Jubei not knowing it, but now she hated him the more for it.

XXIV

"Seikichi, I am surprised at your thought-lessness," said O-Kichi. "You don't care a bit for others. Why don't you tell me everything that happened that night? You are, indeed, narrow-minded. Why, you know it won't make me wild to hear of such a thing. I don't say anything now against my husband, who, making light of me as a woman, keeps everything away from me, but that you should feign ignorance and treat me also as blind and deaf! It is too much for me. You can see easily what is really in my husband's mind, and knowing that, to do nothing but bear him company carelessly in visiting tea-houses, does not give you anything to your credit. And then that you come to visit me like this as if nothing had happened, makes me think you are nothing but wanting. I used to treat you to saké even if my husband was away. But I cannot entertain you to-day. I hate to go into the trouble of making you toasted laver; I cannot bear listening to your foolish gossip. If you want to drink, go yourself to the kitchen and draw from the barrel. If you want somebody to talk with, get a cat for your partner."

So O-Kichi vented her spleen on Seikichi who, ignorant of the real situation, happened to come after the physician was gone. Seikichi on his part was thunderstruck at this sudden volley of her anger, and confusedly asked her what all this was about. On finding gradually what passed between Genta and Jubei at the Horaiya, he confessed his total ignorance of it till then, and sympathized greatly with her in her wrath against Jubei's intolerable act. It was utterly insolent of Jubei, he thought, to reject the exceptional kindness of Genta to whom Jubei owed very much. He could not bear Jubei kick up a dust against his honoured master like that.

"How can I give Jubei a lesson?" he thought in his mind. "Now, my master cannot very well quarrel with Jubei because there is a wide difference in their social standing. If he do, it will be like throwing pearls against stones. So he, I suppose, is forbearing in his anger without letting anybody know his real mind. But why could he not take me into confidence? This is unkind of my master. But, let me see. Here are my master and Jubei, and odds are against the first. But Jubei and I — that is even. Well then. Look out for me, Jubei."

Thus he resolved overhastily in his shallow mind, and turning to O-Kichi, said:

"Forbear me, as there was no help for it, while I was ignorant. But once informed of everything, I shan't remain any longer being lectured to. Just wait and see if I do nothing but bear company with your husband in fooling with girls. I will say sayonara."

He finished excited; and with this he went out, leaving the lattice-door open, and without putting on his sandals, flew away like a wind. O-Kichi felt somewhat uneasy and went out immediately, calling him back once, twice, thrice. And by the fourth time even a shadow of him was not seen any more.

XXV

The scene at the work-yard in the Kannoji compound was liveliness itself. The busy sounds of pattering adzes, of sweeping planes, and of clicking chisels were mingled in the air; the chips flew as withered leaves blown by the wind, and the saw dust danced up and snowed in the clear sky. Here a carpenter, looking smart in a close-fitting working suit of dark blue and in white strapped sandals, was working deftly, and there a day-labourer in a faded dirty coat was seated under an inclined timber and sawing it steadily. Now a gray-haired man was seen whetting his chisel in a sunny place, and then a boy, going hurriedly among chips and shavings, to look for a mislaid tool.

Amidst such a scene of toil, Jubei as master builder was not only superintending all workmen but went himself into the trouble of giving careful instructions whenever any was needed, by word of mouth or in drawing, and Argus-eyed, let nothing pass without his approval. He was now deeply engaged in drawing figures for carving for some workman when who should have appeared but Seikichi, running wilder than a boar and with his face red with anger! Staring at Jubei with his eyes set savagely oblique, he thundered:

"You brute, take it!"

Surprised Jubei looked up, when he saw a hatchet, whetted like a mirror, coming down right on his head, with the fury of a whirlwind. He instinctively dodged, but not until his left ear was severed, and his shoulder was slightly cut. Enraged at his ill-success, Seikichi stepped forward and struck again. Jubei now tried to defend himself, as he receded, by throwing at his opponent a box of nails, a wooden hammer, a ruler, an ink pot, but having no weapon about him, was about to turn and run when he stepped into a toolbox near by and got his foot pierced by a sharp nail. Jubei tumbled unwittingly, and Seikichi, losing no opportunity, raised his hatchet over his head. But no sooner the evening sun lighted the steel and a lightening unknown to the sky flashed than a voice was heard behind him, roaring:

"Fool!"

And both his legs were readily swept off the ground with a log. The man who did this collared Seikichi as he got fiercer for the falling and tried to spring to his feet.

"Here, it is I," said the man. "Fool, come to your senses!"

The hatchet being wrung out of his grasp, Seikichi looked up to the man with eyes big and fiery, lips drawn tight, nostrils bellowing and hair curling at the temples.

"Well," said Seikichi; "is it you, Fire-ball? I have cause to fight. Just leave me alone."

And he struggled impatiently to free himself from the man's grasp. Fire-ball Eiji fixed him by boxing with his knotty fist.

"I'll knock you dead if you stir. You, fool!"

"Let go your hand. That's cruel."

"Fool!"

"You are unreasonable. I cannot let him live, you know."

"Are you crying, fool? I'll knock you more if you don't keep silent."

"You are cruel!"

"Don't cry, fool! I'll knock you dead if you don't."

"You are unreasonable."

"Fool, take that too."

"Let go —"

"Fool!"

"You —"

"Fool!"

"Let —"

"Fool! There at last. Be silent like that. Now, come with me to my house. What, is the fellow dead? How ridiculously weak! Say, fellows, one of you come here. What good can you do now by standing around Jubei like ants while fleeing away at the critical moment? Don't you know Seikichi is now turning into a ghost? Bring some water, you dull-head, and pour it over him. What are you doing with that fallen ear, you stick? Oh, here is water. Don't hesitate; pour the bucketful of it at once over his face. Such a fellow revives easily too. There, Seikichi! Be firm; shame on you to faint! Well now, I'll take this fellow on my back. Jubei hasn't got a deep cut, has he? Well, all right. Sayonara, all you blockheads."

XXVI

"Is Genta in?" said Eiji as he entered the house.

O-Kichi, rising:

"Oh, it is you, Eiji-sama. Come this way, sir."

Eiji passed on to the side of the fire-box and squatted unceremoniously. As he drank half of the cherry-flower water she made him, he said, looking at O-Kichi:

"Is anything wrong with you? You don't look well. Where is Genta? Gone somewhere? You heard the news, I suppose, but Seikichi did a very foolish thing. And I came to talk with you concerning that matter. Well, so Genta went already to Jubei's? That was very quick of him. I feel proud of him to learn that he did that long before I had time to suggest. Why, you have nothing to feel anxious about. All that Genta has to do is to lower his head three or four times to Jubei and the Abbot, and to apologize, saying that it was all from his neglect to instruct his men that Seikichi should do such a rash thing. So you see you need not worry about it at all. But if Jubei is not satisfied with it, why, let Genta take the quarrel upon him and settle it on his own account. Judging from hearsay, I think Jubei himself cannot complain of losing an ear or two for what he got. Maybe this rash act of Seikichi is just a sort of good joke played upon him. But, poor fellow, Seikichi is still groaning from the pain I inflicted with my fist. And then when I told him how the matter would have stood after his killing Jubei, he seemed to feel the full force of his mistake, and was very sorry for his rashness, saying that he did not know what to do in causing Genta to lower his head for his sake. And he was shedding tears pitifully from the thought. He is a nice fellow, isn't he, O-Kichi? Genta may give him a good scolding and even send him to Jubei to apologize. Now, that may not be helped as a matter of form. But there come in your good offices; you will let him — well, you understand the rest, do you? Anyway I'll leave it to you as a woman who is wife to Genta. Ha, ha! I have nothing more to say as Genta is not here. Don't trouble yourself to treat me to-day as I must be going. I shall drop again one of these days. But come and see me any time you want me."

And bidding her good-bye, he returned. O-Kichi, now left alone, mused:

"How I am to blame! Out of the shallowness of my mind, I upbraided Seikichi rashly. The hot-blooded fellow was aroused to do such a reckless thing. The consequence of it is that poor Seikichi is cast into the shade, and my dear husband has to humble himself before that detestable slouch. It came all by accident, but could have been averted if I had been discreet enough. What shall I do now?"

Thus she was buried deep in thought, forgetting herself, till her elbow, with which she supported herself by the fire-box, slipt off the rim.

"Oh, I have it!" she cried at last, and rising, went to her wardrobe. She first took out of a large drawer, fragrant with musk, her obi; one of them, indeed, she girdled herself with at the time of her wedding, two others she had her husband buy for her for their fanciful appeal, and another she prized very much as a gift of her deceased aunt who had once served at a nobleman's house. Her fingers then alighted on her wedding dress. "How innocent I was when I had this on," she thought, but she had to sacrifice it, too. Her other silk dresses attractive in one way or other, — what did she care for to atone, if slightly, for her blunder? She now wrapped them up, and together with a small box in which she placed all her valuable pins and combs, had the maid carry them, while her husband was away, to a pawn-broker's. Taking some money she made in that way, O-Kichi wrapped her head well, and with a small lantern in her hand, started for Eiji's house in the dark night.

XXVII

Genta found it very hard to lower his head and apologize to Jubei whom he now hated as bitterly as he had once loved him much, since their unfortunate meeting at the tea-house, Horaiya. But if he did not take any notice of the recent affair, the reckless act of Seikichi might be construed as done through the instigation of Genta, and the disagreeable scandal might cloud his fame. Morose as he was these days, made more so from the added anxiety on account of Seikichi's foolish act, as he could not very well steer round the rock, without trying to do so, Genta resigned to the inevitable and called upon Jubei reluctantly. He condoled with Jubei on his unlooked-for misfortune, and expressed his regret that he had not given enough counsel to Seikichi. Jubei remained silent as usual; O-Nami gently thanked Genta for his kindness in visiting her wounded husband, and asked him to be at ease as the cut at Jubei's shoulder was fortunately slight. Her words, courteous as they were, struck Genta peculiarly formal, and to his suspicious mind seemed as if hiding thorns somewhere.

"I know their minds without asking," said Genta to himself. "They are suspecting me as a probable instigator of Seikichi. How my heart burns! Oh, let time come soon when I take my revenge upon Jubei in my own way. It will be like anything but the way of a shallow fellow like Seikichi. Do I do such a mean thing as striking an ear off with a hatchet? Is my anger like the burning of shavings which light up easily but are soon reduced to ashes? Accident is accident; my anger is my anger. They are totally different and have no connection whatever. What I do will be known when I do."

Thus displeased as he was, Genta did not show it, and after saying some appropriate words for the occasion, he went at once to the Kannoji, saw the Abbot, and apologized to him for the misdeed of his man. He then came back to his house and was about to go out again to see Eiji, wanting to thank for his interference and to hear more about the matter and to scold Seikichi, who stayed with him, striking eventually the fellow's name from the list of Genta's men. Finding, however, O-Kichi was not in, he questioned the maid about it.

"She went out somewhere, saying that she would be back soon," said the maid, without appearing anything unusual.

Genta, not knowing that she had been hushed, said:

"Oh, did she? Well, tell her when she comes back that I have gone to see Fire-ball Eiji."

And he went out, when he met an old woman coming, supporting her bent body with a bamboo-cane, and carrying an old paper lantern with burnt spots, in her hand.

"Why, aren't you Seikichi's mother?"

"Well, Genta-sama!"

XXVIII

"I am lucky to meet you," asked the woman hurriedly. "But you are going out somewhere, I suppose."

"Well, never mind," said Genta lightly. "Come right in. You wanted to see me, I believe, on some urgent matter, seeing that you ventured out in such a dark night as this."

"Yes, sir: thank you," she answered as she followed Genta and entered the house by the lattice-door. "I am sorry to trouble you so much, but excuse me."

"It's pretty cold, but I am glad to have you call on me. Unfortunately O-Kichi is out, and I cannot very well give you a nice treatment. But come near the fire and make yourself comfortable, without shrinking back in that way."

The woman, making herself still smaller at this kind word of Genta, said; "Thank you, sir; but never mind me. I fear I have already presumed too much on your kindness. I feel quite comfortable here as I have a bosom-warmer."

And she squatted far back near the entrance, wiping with her threadbare sleeve the water off the tip of her nose, that would lodge there in spite of her, and was waiting uneasily for a chance to say something. Genta guessed her mind quickly, and though he was

just on the point of going to Eiji's to meet Seikichi, and loading him with reproaches for his
thoughtlessness, to sever their connection by
way of punishment, he could not help feeling
sorry for his poor mother, who had perhaps
no one she could rely on, except her son and
the Budha, and who, seeing Seikichi thrust
aside by Genta, would feel as if the ground
were cut from under her, and without hope
and consolation, would weep her life to death.
The more he thought of her, the more he pit-
ied her, and was doing nothing but make a
ball of tobacco for his pipe.

The old woman made as if to draw nearer
and began:

"I am sorry to trouble you in the evening.
But I wanted to ask of you some favour. Yes,
sir. You know already, but I heard Seikichi did
such an extraordinary thing. Yes, sir. I heard
it from Tetsugoro-sama, but he is such a hot
fellow that he often frightens me half to death
by his recklessness. He is grown a man under your care, but is still boyish at heart, and
though he never does any crooked things,
but when worked up, he loses his self-control
and causes me a lot of trouble. No, sir; he has
nothing deep-laid. I am glad you know it. I
don't know how he came to pick up a quarrel, but when I heard he brandished a hatchet,
I felt as if I were cut with it. The Chief of Me
Division kindly interposed, I hear. So much

the luckier for him. If he had borne the name of murderer and been condemned to death as such, I could not have lived. Thank you, sir, for your kind words. My son when small was frequently affected with severe convulsions, and I had barely been able to bring him up, praying for the divine favour of Kishimojin-sama. I promised if he recovered to let him go to the shrine and return thanks before he got seven years old. But I neglected to do so by carelessness, and you see him now grown into such a hot fellow, probably for the sin of unfaithfulness. I am sorry he causes you a lot of trouble from time to time. And it was only this afternoon that Tetsugoro-sama brought me the report of his new trouble. I felt as if my breast were rent, when I heard he used his hatchet. I am somewhat at ease to hear that the Chief of Me Division stepped in. But when I asked if Sei got any injury, Tetsugoro-sama did not give me any definite information. He only told me that I should not worry about it. Well, I felt so much the uneasier for that and asked where Eiji-sama's house was. But he could not say if it was all right for me to visit my son, but directed me to you to ask your opinion on that, first of all. After Tetsu-sama's return, my breast ached still more, and I could not keep myself quiet, and so I came to see you, asking the umbrella-mender, my neigh-bour, to look after my house. Please let me

know the house of the Chief of Me Division.
Yes, sir, I intend to go at once. I wish to see
my boy, if he hasn't been hurt badly, to set my
mind at ease if he is doing well, and to hear
more about the matter. I am pretty sure that
he hadn't any mean cause for his deed. But as
he is thoughtless, he might attempt to take his
revenge wrongly. In that case I shall implore
pardon, with tears, from Jubei-sama. I don't
care how much I shall suffer on my boy's account as my days are numbered. But as to my
son who has many, many years yet to live, he
should not incur anybody's ill-will."

So she talked in tears out of her doting love
for her son, without knowing the real story of
the trouble. And Genta was at a loss how to
answer her.

XXIX

"Say, Hachigoro, are you there? Go and open the door; somebody has come," said Eiji.

"Yes, sir," answered the man called, and muttering to himself, "Why, isn't this strange? I hear a woman's voice," he opened the door.

"Come in. But who are you that come at this hour to the woman-hater's house?"

"Thank you, Hat'-san," said the visitor lightly, and blowing off her lantern, began to take off her hood.

Hachigoro watched, and as he found her to be O-Kichi who kindly sent him presents at the customary seasons, he was taken aback and was speedily covering himself up in a heavy quilted gown which he had put on loosely over his body. He hurriedly called to his master inside:

"Master; Mrs. ——, Mrs. —— well, you know."

Eiji, as a true Yedonian who understood all when talked to with a 'you know', said: "Oh, is that so? Come in, O-Kichi. Glad to see you. Sit down anywhere you find least dirty. Take care lest cockroaches should find their way to you. Uncleanliness is the pride of a bachelor's house, you know. So you must bear it with me. If I ever get married to such a nice woman as you, I shall make my house clean."

Eiji laughed, and O-Kichi joined in it, too, saying:

"But then you will perhaps be hating your wife as unclean."

After some such joking, O-Kichi began seriously:

"Is Seikichi sleeping? I want to see how he is."

Eiji, nodding: "Sei has just fallen asleep and doesn't seem to wake up for a while. But he hasn't any wound on his body nor has he got any fracture of his skull. As the surgeon said to-day, he just fainted on being knocked hard when he was very much worked up, and so there is nothing to be anxious about. You can have a look at him if you want to."

O-Kichi followed Eiji and went to a small room where Seikichi was lying sound asleep. Poor fellow! his head and face were all swollen and clearly showed the marks of severe blows. She could not help resenting such a cruel treatment of Eiji, but as it was already a thing of the past, she came back to her seat resignedly, and said to Eiji:

"My husband, being provoked at Seikichi's thoughtless meddling with another's business, will be sure to chastise him severely or to sever his connection with our house or to do some sort of justice in the face of the Abbot and Jubei. But what Seikichi did was not to take his own revenge but rather that of ours, as he thought. He simply got worked up for another's cause. And so I cannot remain merely watching what my husband will do with him. And then I have my own reason why I must do something for him.

"I thought if Seikichi could stay out of town for six months or one year till people cease to gossip about the matter, and my husband will no longer be in ill-humour, I could bridge over easily. So I wanted to send him to the west for a while, and brought with me some money to cover his expenses. It isn't much, but please keep it for him. And when you think fit, give it him with your advice. My husband is such a straightforward man, you know, that he is sure to deal justice to Seikichi whatever he may think of him at heart. He will not change his mind, however Seikichi may cry to him, and I don't see any use of my stepping in if he has to do what justice demands. But I can't remain taking no notice of the trouble he will fall into, you know, doing as he did, not for his own interests. As to his old mother, I will persuade my husband to support her in case her son is away. There is no fear that he will be unreasonable to refuse to do so. But please tell nothing to my husband about my coming here this evening and my favouring Seikichi in secret."

"All right, I understand you," Eiji said. "Oh, you are great. But haven't you anything more to say? Then go back; I expect Genta pretty soon, and it will be rather awkward for you to meet him here."

"Hardly had O-Kichi, encouraged by this blunt but sincere word of Eiji, gone back, thanking him for his favour in anticipation, than Genta called and told Seikichi, as was expected, not to come to his house any more and to think that the relation existing between the two should cease from that moment. Eiji was silent, smiling, and Seikichi cried for mercy. But after Genta returned, Seikichi was made to cry again by Eiji and grunted that he would not depart from the gate of Genta's house even if he were turned into a dog.

A few days after Seikichi, accompanied by Hachigoro, left Yedo for the hot springs of Hakone. He might go from there up the Tokaido route to Kyoto and Osaka, but in his dreams he would return nightly to the city of the east.

XXX

Jubei was getting up early as usual the very next morning of his injury. His wife, being surprised, urged him to give up the attempt.

"Good heavens!" said she, "you to rise this morning! Lie down quiet and don't think of getting out of bed. What will you do if you get lockjaw by exposure this morning? Do lie down still. Hot water will soon be ready; wait till I bring you some and help you with your washing."

And she was throwing some more fuel in the broken range.

Jubei, indifferent to such remonstrance, laughed:

"I need not be nursed as a very sick person. If you just help me wring a wet towel, I rather want to do the rest of the job myself."

And, to the great astonishment of his wife, he filled a small old tub with water and washed himself as usual without any difficulty. Then after finishing his breakfast, he rose and began to change his dress for a working suit.

"How now! Where are you going?" O-Nami wondered. "However much you may think of your work, you cannot afford to neglect what doctor told you. Did he not advise you to keep yourself quiet and to be very careful not to do any rough work till the wound skins over? Why, you have scarcely had time by now for your flesh to come to-gether. But are you going to the Kannoji in spite of that? That is monstrous. You can't work even if you go, and then no one will say anything against you even if you don't. But if you feel uneasy about it, I shall go at once and see the Abbot to get his permission for your staying home three or four days. There is no reason why the all merciful Ab-bot won't give you that; he is sure to tell you to be very careful. Now, come, put on this and stay at home and keep yourself quiet till at least your cut begins to cicatrize."

"Oh, don't meddle with me," said Jubei, and casting aside the clothes O-Nami put over him with his strong right arm, "I don't need this. Give me that haragaké (chest cover)."

"No, you must stay at home," said O-Nami and again tried to cover him with the kimono.

Jubei, thrusting it aside and getting some-what offended:

"What? Are you going to hinder me, you unreasonable woman? I shan't ask your help then. I will dress myself. Don't you think I can discharge my duty of an overseer by stay-ing away even one day on account of such a scratch? You may not know it, but as I am called a fool for my slowness, the workmen are apt to slight me, and though they appear

to work, obeying my instructions, they are secretly idling time away in all sorts of ways,
and none can be found who works honestly.
What a pity! If I tell them to put their best into
their work and to avoid any kind of sham,
they will lower their heads agreeably, but
turning away their faces, laugh at me with
their noses. If I scold, they will speak apolo-
getically but look waxy at me. And if I try to
lead them by gentleness, they will soon get
arrogant. Oh, there is no end to their meanness. It looks very fine to be called by many
as 'Chief' every day, but I am crying in my
heart and feel the life of a mere coolie much
happier than mine.

"Amidst all such troubles, however, I man-
aged in one way or other to push the work
thus far. And so if I take rest to-day, you can't
tell how much it would impede the progress.
Everybody would find some pretext to excuse
him away, and as I could not say anything,
not being there, the work which would otherwise be brought to a speedy finish, would
eventually drag on and get spoiled. In such
an unlucky case, how could I meet the Abbot and Genta? If living I cannot finish the
pagoda, I shall be little less than dead, and
though dead if I can succeed I shall still live.
Can I then lie quiet in bed for such a little cut?
Which do I dread more, lockjaw or the failure
of the work? Though I lose one of my arms, I

must go even if carried till everything comes to a successful finish. Why not then for such a little bit of scratch?"

Saying thus Jubei snatched his haragaké from O-Nami's hand, and trying to put his left arm through, knit his brows. O-Nami could not contradict him now and helped him tenderly to put on his pants and coat. So Jubei set out, leaving his wife agonizing over their unspeakable lot.

At the Kannoji, that morning, the workmen, thinking that Jubei would not be there by any chance, came pretty late, scatteringly. They were greatly astonished at their own mistake, but hardly had they recovered from their surprise than they were accosted by Jubei with 'Glad you don't neglect your work', and sweated with shame. From that time on, however, they gave up their old ways and began to work in earnest. Everything was now done intelligently and with speed. Jubei was hindered in the use of his arm, but for that he gained, as it were, many more arms, and the work progressing rapidly, by the time Jubei's wounds got well, the pagoda was nearly completed.

XXXI

It was toward the end of January. Jubei's toil and exertion had not been wasted, and at last the Shoun Pagoda of the Kannoji Temple was completed successfully. As the scaffolding was removed gradually, the tower discovered itself roof after roof till its whole length of five stories stretched skyward, as if it were a god of might, revealing his frame of one hundred and sixty feet and standing firmly on a rock, defying a host of demons around. How splendidly done! how beautifully finished! unprecedented! unparalleled! — such were the praises everyone showered on the work, from Tameyemon, the secretary, down to the keeper of the gate, forgetting how they first slighted the builder. Nay, some even compared the Abbot and the pagoda, and observed:

"Our Abbot is second to none in our time. There are, indeed, many men of holy orders, high in virtue and profound in learning, but among them he towers matchless even as a lion among the animals or a peacock among the birds. So with the pagoda of this temple; it stands unrivalled, famous as the pagodas at Nara, Kyoto, and at many places in Yedo are. And isn't the contrast beautiful as it is rare in another respect? On the one hand we have the Abbot who picked up a man from the dust where he should have perished without any chance to shine, and who helped him to publish the lustre of his heart of gold, and on the other, Jubei who knew how to be worthy of such a trust, and braving all sorts of difficulty, has at last achieved his object. And the work born out of such concord, — was it done by the hands of men alone or guided secretly by all the good Spirits in Heaven? Stories are told of our famous Tanika-no-Mikoto who was marvelously skilful in building houses, but such a thing was not heard of even in his days, nor was it handed down in the traditions of the Celestial Kingdom. Well then, when the dedication ceremony is held, if you are going to celebrate the occasion by composing a poem, I shall not be behind you to do so by writing an essay in honour of it."

It was well that they should think thus of the occasion and join in the praise of the man's work unselfishly; but unfathomable, indeed, was the will of Heaven!

Yendo and Tameyemon as committee fixed the day for the dedication service. They made out an extensive programme including the grand music service, the dinner given in honour of Jubei and others, the alms-giving to the poor, and the opening of the pagoda for the public. In the midst, however, of the preparation for the occasion, one night the sound of the temple bell fell on the ear unusually dull and muffled. It was a sign of the coming change. Gradually a strange wind began to rise, and as it got so warm that even sleeping children tossed unconsciously their coverings aside, louder rattled the doors along the verandahs, and in the branches of oaks and pine-trees tossed in the dark, the voice of the arch-fiend was heard crying savagely:

"Take peace away out of the hearts of men; strike an awe into the vain and the worldly, and disturb their sleep; heave the waves of blood in the breasts of the shameless; turn the glowing faces of the false pale as ashes. O thou who hast an ax, brandish thy ax. O thou who hast a spear, wield thy spear. Thy sharp swords are hungry; feed them with food. There is no better food than the flesh and the blood of men; feed then thy swords with the flesh to the full. To the full let them drink in the blood."

No sooner was the command given than all at once a fierce tempest broke, and at the same time the demons with axes, the demons with spears, and the demons with hungry swords, all began to run riot.

XXXII

The young and the old within the six miles
square of the city of Yedo were all awakened
from their dreams, and alarmed and crying
that the evil wind had come, made a great
confusion, fastening the doors and tighten-
ing the bars. The arch-fiend, however, taking
no pity on them, raised his angry voice again:

"O ye demons, never shrink from men, but
let them shrink from you. Men have slighted
us, have mocked us long, have neglected to
offer regular offerings due to us. Dogs which
go standing instead of on all fours, fowls
which build their nests of pride and lust,
monkeys which have no tails, snakes which
can talk, sons of foxes which are all lies and
deceits, daughters of swines which know no
filth — they have scoffed at us: can we bear
them any longer? Can we leave them longer,
taking pride in scoffing at us? We bore them
as long as we could; as long as we could we
left them scoffing at us. Sixty-four years of
patience have already past. I have broken
asunder the chain of fortune that bound us; I
have split the rock of mercy that imprisoned
us. Then rush on, and tear wild; now is your
time. Punish them and punish at once for
the wrongs they did us for years. Seize their
stinking pride and cast it into the pit; let their

heads bow to the ground. Try in their breasts the sharpness of your ruthless spears; gash their cheeks with your cruel axes and wrathful swords; strike their throats with your icy steels and make them tremble with keen anguish; pierce their hearts and let them convulse with inner spasm. Kill before their eyes many sons and daughters of lust they gave birth to, and bury away their unclean thoughts into the sea of sighs and remorse. They robbed silkworms of their houses; rob them then of their houses. They laughed at the sagacity of the silkworm, laugh then at their sagacity. Deride their thought they admit to be great, their device they hold to be clever, their sense they believe to be sound, their feeling they think to be refined, and their strength they regard as powerful. All they have is for your spears, for your axes, for your swords; so deride it first and feed your weapons with it and laugh at them who provide you with such good provisions. Don't murder men at once but kill them by inches and do so as long as possible. Whip them with scorpions; skin them alive; tear their flesh; make balls of their hearts and kick them up. The heaving of sighs, the shedding of tears, the beating of hearts, the crying of pain, — stop them all and take them all out of men. There is no pleasure but cruelty for us, and if ye are not cruel, ye are none of us.

"Then rush on, rush wild. Lawless and heartless, run wild, run riot. Fight even with gods; knock down even budahs. Tear down reason and crush it, and then the world will be ours."

As the arch-fiend spurred his army, millions of demons danced for joy, throwing sand and stones, and never ceasing from the middle of the night till the morning; and those who rushed over the sea tossed the waves up, and those who dashed on land kicked up the dust, darkening the light of the sun and filling the heaven and earth with yellow clouds. Some, brandishing their axes, cut off, laughing, the pine-trees which were tenderly cared for in a rich man's garden; some, wielding their spears, tore open wooden roofs in no time; and some, with marvelous strength, shook bridges and firmly built houses.

"Not quite; put in more of your vim. Follow me."

Crying thus and gnashing his teeth, the arch-fiend stamped with rage and impatience when the evil spirits that filled the air, yelled and shrieked and raged recklessly; and as the trees in the compounds of shrines and temples as well as around the palaces of the rich, screamed and wailed, straining the voices, the willows and the bamboos stood on end like the hair, then swayed, and were torn.

By this time the black clouds had flooded the sky, and the rain as big as nuts began to fall. The demons, infuriated still more, did not lose time to pull down fences, break gates, tear off roofs, and kick off tiles. On the first attack, they blew off a cottage; on the second they wrenched an upper story away; on the third they crushed a temple successfully. With shouts and roars like the rolling of waves, they disquieted and frightened men, laughed at the comicality of their anxiety and confusion, and rejoiced at the grief of those who lost their shelters.

As the demons threatened to rage still more, tens of thousands of people living in the eight hundred and eight streets of Yedo, were terror-stricken and were turned pale as ashes. And among those startled especially were Endo and Tameyemon.

The pagoda just finished with such pains was rocking in the wind, its spire swayed, and the ball on the top of it described a strange character in the sky. As the blast that might have sent a rock rolling, struck it, and the rain that might have pierced a shield, dashed against it, the tower bent and creaked, and no sooner did it straighten itself than it bent and creaked again, threatening every minute to fall down.

"Look, how dangerous!" cried they. "Can nothing be done to prevent the pagoda from falling? It would be an irretrievable blow if it should. But as there are no trees around, the tower, with such a small basis for its height, can hardly hope to stand in this tempestuous weather. See how this temple shakes! How much more then with the pagoda! Is there no charm to stop the wind? Hasn't Genta come who ought to visit us to see if anything goes amiss in such a storm? And Jubei, — his connection with the Kannoji is quite recent, but he cannot escape being blamed for it if he does not come. Can he remain unconcerned for the pagoda he built while even others feel ill at ease for it like this? Look, how dangerous! It is bending again! Let some one go and call Jubei."

And they searched for a man to do the errand, but no one dared to go through falling tiles and shooting stones. At last, however, Hichizo, the old odd man, was secured for the service for a good sum of money.

XXXIII

Covering his head with a hood and tying a broad-rimmed bamboo-hat over it to keep the rain off, and putting on a heavy rain-coat and strapping it well about the waist, old Hichizo, with a strong cane in his hand, forced his way in fear through the violent storm, and reached Jubei's house at last. To his great astonishment, he found that half the roof of the house was ruthlessly blown away, and that father, mother, and son, huddled pitifully in a corner, were barely able to keep off with old mats the splashes of rain-drops falling from the ceiling. Struck with the much-talked-of dull-wittedness of Jubei, which verged upon helplessness, he turned to tell his errand:

"Say, Jubei-dono, you should not stay like that in such a storm, should you? Outside it is just like a battle scene; tiles are flying about, and trees are blown down. And in such a din and confusion what do you think of the pagoda you built? It's so high, has nothing around it and stands on such a narrow foundation that it is struck violently by the wind from every direction, and is shaken terribly and bent like a flag pole. And as it does so and creaks furiously, both Endo-sama and Tameyemon-sama are terribly shaken, fearing that it will fall down every minute. Properly speaking, you ought to come out without being asked to do so; but isn't this too cool of you to remain indifferent to this extraordinary weather? So on your account I had to come on a dangerous errand, and look here, my goodness! I got such a lump. My hat was blown off; the rain soaked me to the skin; and as ill luck would have it, a piece of wood came flying and struck me on the forehead. But come along with me. Tameyemon-sama and Endo-sama instructed me to fetch you. How now! I am amazed: the door has been blown away! Well, you see, you can't tell how long the pagoda can remain secure. It may fall down while I am talking. So get up quick; make haste."

As he urged Jubei, O-Nami put in her word anxiously:

"If you go, as it is very dangerous on the way, you'd better put on that heavy hood, old and rotten as it is. I will take it out, so have that on. There is no knowing something will hit you. And put on that heavy overcoat, too, though it is all rags. You have no time to think of your appearance."

Jubei, rather displeased, looked sharply toward his wife, who was going to open a closet, and said:

"Oh, don't trouble yourself about them. I am not going; I don't see any reason to stir about even if it blows hard." Calmly to the old man, without so much as turning about: "Hichizo-dono, I thank you for your trouble, but the pagoda is all right. It is not so frail as to come to the ground in this kind of weather. So there is no need of my going out. You tell to Endo-sama and Tameyemon-sama that as it is all right, they need not trouble themselves about it at all."

"Well, but at any rate come along with me," said Hichizo, rather offended at Jubei's manner. "You'd better come and see how the pagoda quakes and creaks. You can say a bold thing here, without looking at it, but if you see it nodding like a flag pole, inexcitable as you are, I am sorry to say, you will find your heart failing you. There is no use in bragging here. Come along with me quick. There, another blast! How fearful! It does not look to stop soon. I am sure, Endo-sama and Tameyemon-sama are awaiting us with impatience; come out then, putting on your hood or coat or anything."

"No, you go back, feeling easy. The pagoda is all right," replied Jubei bluntly.

"No, I cannot be at ease so readily," replied Hichizo obstinately.

"The pagoda is all right," Jubei assured him again.

Hichizo, now growing impatient, said roughly:

"Come with me whether you will or not. It is not my word but the command of Endo-sama and Tameyemon-sama, mind you."

Jubei was now somewhat offended and said:

"I beg your pardon but it was not by Endo-sama or Tameyemon-sama that I was ordered to build the pagoda. But the Abbot, I presume, did not send you for me on account of the storm. He did not do such an inconsiderate thing, did he? If the time should come when the Abbot, too, would say 'Go and call Jubei; the pagoda is dangerous,' I will lose no time to hurry to the temple, because it would be a great moment for me, — the moment in which the fate of my life hangs. But until he does not doubt my work a whet, you have nothing to fear. There is no trick in my work, no sham, no dishonesty; so whatever others may say of it, it stands with ease in the rain and in the wind just as in calm weather. So I don't fear a storm or an earthquake at all. You go and tell so to Endo-sama, please."

Thus bluntly told by Jubei, Hichizo had nothing to do but to go back through the storm to the Kannoji. He told all about Jubei to Endo and Tameyemon, when one of them said:

"Why, you old tactless fellow. Why don't you tell Jubei that the Abbot wanted him to come? Look, how the tower quakes! You got to be slow like Jubei, perhaps through his influence. There is no help then; go again and bring him here by all means, pretending that it is the Abbot who wants him."

Scolded thus severely, Hichizo muttered something disconsolately but went again out of the temple gate.

XXXIV

"Now, Jubei, you must come by all means," cried old Hichizo pantingly before entering Jubei's house. "I won't let you say anything against the order this time. It is the Abbot who wants you."

"What?" said Jubei, getting up no sooner than he heard the word. "The Abbot wants me, do you say? Is it possible, Hichizo-dono? Alas the day! It makes me cry to think that, however strong the wind may be, the Abbot whom I trust completely should take, too, what I have built with my whole soul as something frail and unstable. Yes, I trusted him as the only one in the world, a god, a budha, who looked at me with merciful eyes and judged me rightly. But hasn't my work appeared even to him as solid? Oh! what a hopeless world this is! There is no use of my living any longer. I rejoiced at being known luckily to the one unparalleled in these days for piety and for depth of learning, and held it as my greatest honour, but the joy has been empty and short-lived as a dream, and ends thus in being doubted if that pagoda I took so much pains to erect may come down for a puff of wind! How provoking! Am I really such a worthless, shameless fellow not to be able to give stability to my work, or even if it could not stand the test and were disgraced, to live on just wiping the sweat of humiliation off my forehead? O-Nami, do I appear to be such a mean fellow to you? I don't care any more for my life; am disgusted with myself. Being slighted and cast aside by the world, the longer I live, the more I have to suffer mortification. Well then, let the storm grow harder; let the pagoda come down. For mercy's sake let even a slight damage be done to it. As the wind and the rain are not half as heartless to me as men, I may feel glad, but certainly do not bear a grudge to them, to have the tower ruined. Of course, in case a piece of board be blown off or even a nail get loose, as I have nothing to expect in this world, I shall kill myself straightway. People would then say of me: 'A fool by the name of Jubei brought disgrace on himself on account of the slovenness of his work, but he was not such a mean fellow as to live on because he wanted to.' I must give up my life sometime, and this is just the right place and moment to do so. I rather hesitate to defile the holy ground, but how can I go away from the place if the pagoda standing there should be ruined? Forgive me, O Budahs, but let me end my life by casting myself down from the top of the Shoun Pagoda. My body will be torn and make an ugly show, but it contains nothing foul in it. Pity me, the blood I spill is the pure blood of a straightforward man!"

Jubei got excited: he said this half to himself, and while saying he went out and walked on as in a dream, even losing Hichizo somewhere on the way, and arrived, as if unexpectedly to him, at the pagoda.

Going up the stairs inside, Jubei now reached the uppermost floor, and opening the door, thrust half his body out when the rain struck him in the face like pebbles, preventing him from opening his eyes, and the wind so fierce that it seemed as if to carry off the one ear left to him, took his breath away. He unwittingly drew a step back, but mustering his courage, he pushed out and stood grasping the railing firmly. The sky was darker than the blackest night, and only the angry noise of the tempest filled the air. Firm as it was, the tall pagoda swayed as often as a strong blast came dashing, and rocked helplessly like a boat tossed on wild waters. Jubei was not a little surprised at this though fully prepared for it, but thinking that the greatest crisis of his life would come at any moment, he stared into the darkness, gnashing his teeth, and straining every nerve in his body, stood grasping tightly the handle of a chisel he had brought for the occasion, and waited calmly for his fate.

There was, however, a strange man, unobserved by Jubei, going round and round the pagoda, braving the storm.

XXXV

There was a general talk in the town about the storm when it was over. Even old men, who in case anything happened were never tired of telling about a similar incident occurring some twenty or thirty years ago as something far more terrible, confessed that it was the fiercest they ever had in their lives while younger jesting folk who always found a good topic to talk on in natural calamity, gossiped about others' misfortune over tea, making merry with the blowing off of the attic of such and such a house or the crushing of the watch-tower at such and such a person's ground, having no fear of incurring anybody's displeasure.

"Look at so and so," one of them would say. "Isn't it very like him to invest foolishly in that sort of a theatre out of his greediness and to be payed out like that? But how ridiculously complete that ruin of the house is! And that haughty professor in flower arrangement, living in the side street over there, hasn't he been given a lesson to by having the upper story of his house blown off? But do you know why that new temple, one of the largest in Yedo, has fallen down so easily? A large sum of contribution was raised from the parishioners to build it, but also a good

deal of appropriation on the part of the officers and tricks of the contractors and the like
went along with the work of erection, I hear.
Maybe those big pillars in the chapel were
nothing but empty barrels."

Everybody, however, could not help expressing his admiration on the workmanship
of the Shoun Pagoda at the Kannoji Temple,
that not a nail was loosened nor a board was
dislodged in the storm.

"Well, but what a strong-willed man that
Jubei is who built the pagoda!" one observed.
"They say that he was determined not to live
if the pagoda came to the ground. He was
upon the tower, I hear, grasping the railing
and staring at the storm, ready, in such a great
commotion, to jump headlong one hundred
and sixty feet, with a chisel in his mouth. I
think the pagoda could not be shaken down
just for that will of his. Maybe the god of wind
could not go on with his damaging work, being looked at sharply as he was by Jubei's
blood-shot eyes. Isn't he a real master builder,
the like of whom has not been found since
the days of Jingoro? The pagoda at Shiba and
Asakusa were damaged to some extent, but
the fact that the Shoun Pagoda did not incline
even a tenth of an inch argues superb crafts-
manship, doesn't it?"

"Well, I heard another story about the pagoda," remarked another. "The master of

that Jubei must be a great fellow, too. He was
going round and round the pagoda, soaking in the heavy rain to see if it did not suffer even a slight damage from the storm. He
intended that in case it did, he would rebuke
Jubei severely for it, saying that he brought
shame on his friends and disgrace to the
rest of the builders, and that he had nothing to pay with but his death, and so driving him to the same sort of circumstance as
in the case of a samurai to commit hara-kiri,
till the humiliated Jubei could not take up
his tools again."

"No, that fellow is not master to Jubei but
his rival in trade, I hear," corrected a third,
knowingly.

On the day the ceremony, celebrating the
completion of the pagoda, after being post-
poned on account of the storm, was at last
performed, the Abbot invited Genta on purpose and went up the tower with him and Jubei. Taking a writing brush his page had carried there by his special order and soaking it
with ink, he said to the two men:

"Look here, Jubei and Genta. I will write on
the pagoda what ought to be inscribed after."

And in a bold hand, he wrote,"
Built by Jubei of Yedo
and
Completed by Gentaro Kawagoye,
On the — day of — — —"

As the Abbot, his face all smiles, turned and looked on them, the two could not say a word but only bowed their heads reverentially in token of the deepest joy and gratitude.

Since then the sacred pagoda has stood high to the sky; when seen from the west, sometimes the white moon climbed over it, and when viewed from the east, of evenings the red sun tinted the tiles and the railings. And *it is now* more than one hundred years since the erection, *but* the story *still lives* fresh in the hearts of men.